To Christine
From
Thanks

From Clare to Texas

Launched 3·7·2010

Margaret Dowling

Copyright © Margaret Dowling, 2009

First Published in Ireland, in 2009,
in co-operation with Choice Publishing,
Drogheda, County Louth, Republic of Ireland
www.choicepublishing.ie

ISBN: 978-1-907107-30-6

All rights reserved. No part of this publication may be reproduced, stored in a retrieval system, transmitted in any form, or by any means, electronic, mechanical, photocopying, recording or otherwise, without the prior permission of the copyright holder.

Table of Contents

About the Author	i
Authors Note	ii
Acknowledgements	iii
Preface	iv

Part 1	
Reminiscings	1
Mary's Ambitions	3
Old School Hall Ceílí	5
Mary is Employed in the Woollen Mill	6
Brid Knitting	7
The Romance	8
Big Disappointment	10
Let Down	12
Dad Passes Away	13
Brid Starts to Knit Again	15
My First Ceílí	16
My Twenty First	18
Emigration Plans	19
Going to Dublin	22
On the Train Coming Home	24
Sharing a Joke	25
Breaking the News	26
Mam Makes a Stand	28
A Solution	30
American Wake	32
Hiding the Visa	33
A Visit to Father Clancy	34
The Will	35
Last Good Bye's	36
Sad Partings	37
Arriving in Queens Town	38
Nora Shortens the Time	39
Exploring the Liner	41
Disembarking	45
First Texan Meal	46
Accommodation	48
The Rub Down	50
New Positions	51
A Good Cry	52
Discussing the New Positions	53
Ranch Owners	54
The Ho-Down	55

Getting a Man	57
A Spectacular Beauty	58
Letter Writing	60
Pay Day	61
Wedding Plans	62
Mary's Wedding Day	64
Another Wedding	67
Nora and Mary have a Chin Wag	69
Elsa's Past	70
An Emotional Feeling	73
Lying in State	75
Last Journey	76
Funeral Mass	78
Reminiscing	81
Joan has her Baby	82
Jake Óg's Christening	83
Final Get Together	85
Mam's Letter	87
We have a Son	89
Father Clancy's Reply	90

Part 2

Donnald Goes to Ireland	91
Donnald's Surprise	92
An Irish Dinner	93
Donnald Arrives in Ireland	94
Donnald Loses his Way	96
Finding Hospitality	97
Eileen's Thoughts	100
Bess has Twins	102
Photographing the Twin Calves	105
The Hundred Pound Note	107
Donnald on the Road Again	109
Bathing in the Mill River	110
Meeting Aunt Brid	111
Aunty gives Eileen's History	113
The Plan	114
Aunty tells of the Escape	115
Mick Proposes	117
Mick and Eileen arrive in Dublin	119
Wedding Breakfast and Gifts	121
Eileen's Dad in a Rage	122
Then the Guards came	124
Donnald's Explanation	126
Eileen's Spending Spree	127
Revisiting the Pub	128

Dad took to the Bottle	130
Eileen hears about her Sisters Marriages'	132
Donnald takes more Photos	133
Passion	136
Eileen in Charge	137
Mick reveals his Background	138
Donnald meets Father Tomson	139
Small World	141
Donnald heads North	143
Meeting his Father's Family	144
A Night in Donnald's Honour	146
Goodbyes and Hellos	148
Aunty Breathes her Last Breath	150
Eileen feeling Dizzy	151
Surprise for Eileen	152
Donnald goes Home to Texas	155
First Day back at Work	156
An Irish Film Premier	157
Eileen in Labour	159
Eileen has few Visitors	161
Mick feeds his Baby Son	163
Eileen sends Word to her Sisters	164
Sisters helping Out	165
A Nostalgic Irish Film	167
Donnald Upset	168
A Nasty Rumour	169
Eileen meets her Brother	171
A Necessary Return	172
Signing the Paper	175
Another Fright	176
Mrs Ryan has her Say	177
Mick a new Man	180
We're Back	181

About the Author

My imagination was fuelled for storytelling, having being reared by my grandmother in a little white washed cottage, where neighbours came to sit around the open turf fire on winter nights in the little village of Kilnacree, County Clare.

Turf fire smoke and pipe smoke were some of the satisfying aromas that I can still remember of that time. But with the passing of Granny, my dear mother took me home to Galway, where I lived and went to school with my three siblings. Nothing was ever the same.

My next venture was emigration to New York City, where I met and lived with my Aunt for a period of time. I worked through the loneliness – grin and bear were my passwords.

A few years after arriving in New York, I met and fell in love with a lovely Irish man named Michael Beggen. We married and had two beautiful sons. Unfortunately time with Michael was short, and sad to say our happy life came to a heartbreaking end with his sudden death. I returned to Galway to rear my two sons.

After a period of time, I met Paddy Dowling, a widower with two children. We married and had two daughters together. We had nineteen years of a happy marriage, and then Paddy passed away suddenly. Once more, I became a widow.

Now in my mature age, I am happily passing my time putting pen to paper by writing poetry and short stories. This is my preliminary novel; I do so hope you will enjoy reading it.

Authors Note

This book is a work of fiction; all of the characters are fictional, as are the scene locations. Emigration itself is very real and true to life. I have tried as best as my memory allows, bringing to light the hardships of emigration in the late 1800's and early 1900's and allowing the story to be near present time as can be noted by the manner of which in travelling overseas.

Though some of the events, within this story, that occurred came from Mary's reminiscing and how emigration affected some individual family members through disappointment, heartbreak that would linger in one's own mind down the years in a deafening silence.

In part two of the story, the young Texan is seeking to locate his roots on both sides of his house. He encounters both sadness and happiness in equal measures. He has come to the conclusion that only in America could the rich and poor people connect faithfully for better or worse.

Inspiration was derived from some of my own relations who experienced emigration, plus my own Aunt who sponsored me out to New York in the 1950's, sadly some of these memories have died along with my relatives.

Acknowledgements

A special thank you to my awesome family, for their incomparable love and support, especially Margery who patiently proof read every single word and Caroline for making the necessary modifications and corrections.

I would like to express a deep appreciation to the Ballybane Resource Centre, especially Martina Derrane for her wonderful assistance in typing and providing sample layout for my finished story.

A sincere thank you to the staff of the Ballybane Library, for their continual support and guidance.

Also, not to overlook the people who fed me an ocean of inspiration to my already over flowing mind, to facilitate the completion of this story.

Cover photo was taken with model wearing original coat and suitcase used around 1952, the time when the Irish people were immigrating to America.

Back cover is an original passport of that period – 1952.

The dedication of this book is in the memory of my family who immigrated to various parts of the world in the 19th Century.

Preface

This story of emigration takes in different decades of the Twentieth Century, the poor times of Ireland. Parts of Ireland at that time were more poverty stricken than other parts, as the reader will discover.

The chief characters of the story are three young girls growing up together in a little remote village in Ireland. Taking daily life as it came to them, until the emigration bug hit one of them. America was the way forward to a better life.

Mary O'Brien, the chief character in the story is in her senior years and many times she lapses into past life, reminiscing of the times gone by. She reprimands herself back to reality and the present day.

The three young girls, good friends as there were, set sail to make find their fortune in the foreign land, where they encountered disappointment, conflict, sadness along with a little comedy in the passage of their lives.

If the pace seems a little slow at times, do not despair for there are surprises just around every corner with twists and turns, highs and lows, best not to divulge too much at this point, but do enjoy the story as it unfolds.

The characters and places are fiction of the writers imagination, names and places bear no resemblances to any person living or dead.

Part One

Reminiscings

Mary is reminiscing on her past life. 'Tis a good many years now' she said to herself 'since I left that ould sod'. Her good husband passed away after twenty five years of a happy marriage. Donnald, their pride and joy, which was an only son, has grown up into a handsome young man, working in a top accountancy firm. The story unfolds as follows:

In another year or so himself and Madeline, will join their hands in holy matrimony, yes indeed, America has without a shadow of a doubt been good to her. She most certainly has done well. 'Why now'? Mary asks herself whilst sitting in her comfortable modernised kitchen with every conceivable electrical appliance invented to make work about the kitchen easy. Why should she be feeling this empty void called loneliness?

Looking out at the vast expanse of land, which was now all hers and, of course Donnald's. Thinking back on that remote home place, it was certainly the most dreary places consisting of backward hamlets. In her minds eye, she could see her sister Brid and herself, in the little thatched cottage with the swirl of smoke coming up out of the little chimney, you could tell the direction the wind was blowing by the curve it took. Happy times with mam and dad, the little farm of land that kept them in comfort, their dad worked hard keeping it cultivated. Brid was a good eight years older than me, she said to herself, as children, many a time I would call Brid to come and play a game with me 'I can't come now' she would answer 'I'm helping mammy', or so it seemed.

Brid missed a lot of days from school due to helping mammy with jobs around the house. Mary making excuses to the teacher telling her that Brid has a sore throat, or she has a pain in her side. The teacher would question Mary, 'Is Brid delicate Mary? Did mammy take her to the doctor? What did he say'? "I don't know Miss', Mary would whisper with her head down. There were times she would hear Brid complaining, 'Mam why don't you keep Mary home from school to help you with the work? I don't like missing school'. Mam would cajole her by saying 'Now Brid dear, there's a good girl, Mary is not near as good at 'elping me with these chores as you are, anyway she's only a young un'. Thinking back to them years so long ago, a lonely feeling swept over Mary, the tears began to flow. Oh! Dear, living in this beautiful place can sure bring it's moments of desolation. Springhope Texas was indeed a far cry from the euphoria of the times in Ballygala, Co. Clare.

Growing up together Brid and herself shared a lot of sisterly secrets, how close they were then sharing plans and dreams, the space of years made no difference to them.

From Clare to Texas

Mary's Ambitions

Mary confided one of her ambitious dreams to Brid one evening, as they carried buckets of water from the well. Laying down the buckets to give their weary arms a rest, Mary blurted out 'I'm going to America Brid, earn the dollars, send some home to mam and dad and parcels of nice clothes to you Brid'. 'Well indeed Mary, you won't ever see America' was Brid's surprise reply. 'People heading out yonder must 'ave a relative to pay their way, and be responsible for them too out there Mary. Sure didn't olde Mrs O'Neill tell me all about it the other Sunday on me way home from Mass, her daughter Vera wouldn't 'ave had a chance of going, only for her big Uncle Tom, her fathar's brother, and let me tell you something else' Brid says taking a gulp of air, 'All them papers you 'ave to fill in, and then there's the permission letter thing from your parents, and a letter from our lovely Parish Priest, and a character reference from the Garda. Then you'll 'ave to go to Dublin to the American Embassy to be asked all sorts of questions by them big fellas from America and Doctors examining you. I tell you Mary, there's a lot of preparation of going to America. Indeed Mary, you haven't a chance of going. Sure we have no-one belonging ta us over there'. 'The best thing for you to do now that you're finished school Mary is apply for a job in the local woollen mill'. Picking up the buckets we walked slowly along the path, still talking as to what I should do, Brid giving me her older sisterly advice. I hate the thought of working in the woollen mill, but I suppose it is what I will have to do.

'There's nothing else around 'ere to do unless, that is of course you go into the city, that's over ten miles away, get a job there, and you would 'ave to stay in digs, that would cost money. You know yourself Mary how much mam and dad will be depending on your earnings for the house. As for me, they depend on me to help them, both indoors and outdoors with the work. I can't find it in me heart to leave them and go out to work. I've missed a lot of time from school, never getting the same schooling as you Mary, I'm twenty three years o' age, and sure what do I know? Only rough farm work, and a bit o' knitting and sewing'. 'Oh dear Brid, don't run yoursel' down, sure you're a great knitter; I love to listen to the click of your knitting needles flying between your fingers. You can knit up a mans' geansai in three nights. Didn't I see you knitting the lovely navy blue one for dad? If I get the job in O'Flynns Woollen Mill maybe I can buy a hank o' wool cheap for you. You could knit a variety of garments to sell, make a bit of money for yourself'. 'Thanks Mary, that's great encouragement from me baby sister'. 'Brid, I'm almost all grown up too, you know'. We both had a good laugh.

'All that knitting would take up a lot of time, I would be no sooner seated than dad would need me outside to help him, or mam would have a job inside for me to do, and that would be me put the knitting aside for much, much later. Indeed Mary, my life is no way me own with them two'. 'Ah Brid', I coax, 'Don't be too hard on them, sure they're getting olde'.

Old School Hall Ceílí

Mary was trying to work out a plan to get Brid out of the house for a night. I reminded her of the ceílí in the old school hall on Sunday night. 'It's going to be a great night Brid, why don't you go? I can bet John Kelly will be there, you know you had a crush on him'. 'Yes' answered Brid, 'Me and every girl in the parish of Ballygala'. 'Never mind them; you look so pretty in your navy floral dress with the lace collar'. 'Floral dress is it? Sure it's the only rag I have. At the same time, I think I might as will go. He might be at this big ceílí too; if he is I hope he gives me a couple o' dances' said an unmoved Brid. 'Make a play for him and I bet he will bring you home. I'll be awake when you get in, sure I'll be dying to hear all the news' said Mary trying to get Brid into the mood for dancing and having a bit of fun. 'Go on with yoursel' Mary you'll make a good match maker someday' Brid added.

Mary is Employed in the Woollen Mill

Getting hired on at the mill was easier than imagined, Mary thinking to herself. 'You start Monday morning Mary O'Brien' said the Manageress. 'Here's your card, you sign it each morning here in my office and again when you're finished work and always put the time on it. Your uniform will be here for you Monday morning'. 'Thank you Miss O'Flynn' Mary managed to say to the stern manageress.

I remember I was both nervous and excited on that Monday. Signing in, getting the uniform; which was a dark navy, heavy and rough, but at least it protected our own clothes from the oil of the wool. Even now my head aches remembering the noise of the mill wheel and the fast gushing of the water as it kept the wheel turning for the washing of the wool. I thought I would never get used to it. It was hard work combing each piece of wool. The laugh and the crack with the other workers made time pass fast. All tools down, uniforms off, hung on rusty nails driven into the wall, where your name was scribbled over it. Everyone dashed for the door as the loud hooter sounded for quitting time, some people would remain behind working late. What memories I have of that mill. Collecting our pay envelope each Friday, the pay master would ask if we wanted a hank or two of wool, it would be deducted from the next weeks pay envelope at only half the price, 'a good way to make yourself a cheap cardigan' he would laugh. I was thrilled to be able to provide Brid with a couple of hanks each week.

Brid Knitting

Brid was knitting every chance she got. She knitted everything from gloves, mittens, hats, and scarves, to geansai's. She was a dab hand at it. The needles going so fast you could see, almost seeing sparks coming from them. Now at last Brid was starting to save a bit of money in the post office for herself.

One day mam took me one side and said 'Mary, unless Brid gives you the price of the wool from now on, you'd be best cut back on it, the house needs your wages. She's taking some orders now from people, so she can afford it.' 'Alright mam' I said, with some doubt in my mind.

Strangely it worked out, that maybe Brid overheard what mam said to me for the next order of wool she wanted, she gave me the price of it. Of course I knew the people she knitted for paid her a little off each week, and still she turned out beautiful work. I loved to sit and watch her. As for me, I couldn't cast on a stitch. Brid could knit rope stitch, moss stitch, garter stitch and many more. I think what I liked best of all was the intricate way she could mix and match colours into fairisle patterns, knit cardigans, jumpers and waistcoats in every size. She could have made a lot more money if she was paid in full upfront instead of the customers paying her on the cuff saying candidly to her 'that's all I can give you this week Brid, I'll have a bit more for you next week'. Brid kept a little book to record customer names' and payments in it.

The Romance

I was dying to hear all about the new romance between herself and John. My thoughts repeatedly consisted of how were they progressing in their courtship? 'How are you and John getting on'? I asked Brid one day, trying to keep from exploding. 'Oh! John', she says, 'John's a great set dancer. We hammer the boards every Sunday night Mary', Brid replied ever so calmly. 'Now aren't you glad I suggested for you to doll yourself up that Sunday night for that local ceilí. How long ago is it now'? I asked excitedly. 'Three years now Mary, as long as you've being working in that woollen mill'. 'That length, eh'? I gasped 'Any sign of a proposal? (Mrs Kelly) I could get used to calling you Mrs Kelly' I chuckled. 'Oh Mary, where would John and I live? I'm stuck here and I can't see a way out. John has his own troubles, even though he is their one and only, he has a hard enough time trying to please that cranky ould father of his, never mind bringing a woman into their house. It's a lovely house; they've a lovely neat kitchen, and very good land. I wonder sometimes what he sees in me'? 'Brid', I shouted at her, 'You are the finest looking girl in these parts, don't run yourself down'. Sitting thinking of the chats my sister and I used to have sharing our every thought, what pleasant times they were.

'How about yourself Mary, any dates with the handsome mill boys coming up'? Brid enquired one day. 'Brid for goodness sake, it's bad enough working with them scruffy oily boys and apart from that you know what mam would say if she thought I was going out on a date', 'You're not eighteen years yet, too young to be looking at boys, your sister was nearly twenty one when she went out to her first ceilí, even then she had to be home by eleven o'clock or your dad wouldn't let her out again' 'Would be the words mam would drum at me Brid'.

Recalling that conversation Mary's thoughts went back to Brid telling her how she watched the hall clock and praying that the hour hand wouldn't travel so fast. 'How I enjoyed those sets she would say, enjoyed them to the hilt Mary'. One day out of curiosity, I asked Brid if the savings were building up in her post office book, 'Surely yourself and John must be making some progress to give us a big day, I'm dying to be a bridesmaid'. 'Have a bit of sense Mary', she says, 'I'm going to be stuck here for many a day yet, God forgive me, I don't mean it the way it sounds. There is something going on in Kelly's, I'm going to tell you about it, don't breath a word to a soul, promise me Mary'. 'I promise'. Looking at Brid I never before seen such a strain in her face, 'What's the matter', I asked? Brid was never one to gossip, I couldn't imagine what could have her in such a state.

Margaret Dowling

Big Disappointment

At the last Fair held in Clover Town, John held out to get a good price for his six head of cattle, holding out to the very last he knew the man was keen to buy so kept slapping hands until the final deal was agreed. John's dad just stood around listening to the two men bargaining, John felt proud to win out with his fine bullocks. After the fair John and his dad went home. The mother had a fine breakfast waiting on the table for them, rashers, eggs, black pudding, her lovely homemade bread sliced onto a plate, a big pot of tea, and the home churned butter. Now she said 'My two hardworking men, sit in there and tuck in'. Sitting in to the table John was bursting to count out the money. Tossing it onto the table, 'Look at that dad, them bullocks brought a fine price dis morning. Enough to put down payment on that tractor I've been talking about to cut down the workload'. The money was lying in the middle of the table. 'It's a nice price to get alright', says the dad, 'but not for a tractor' and with that he reached out, gathered up all the money and shoved it into his own pocket and not as much as a shilling did he give poor John.

'I can tell you Mary there was no breakfast eaten in that house that morning and the poor mother, yes the poor mother, she went out the door drying her eyes in her apron, and went as far as she could up the garden in the way she wouldn't hear the terrible words passing between father and son.

'But Brid that Fair was held over a month ago', I managed to say in shock. 'I know Mary and neither father nor son, have spoken a word to each other since. As for poor John he has no ambition for anything now. He is as white as a ghost, his mother keeps saying, 'be patient your dad will come around John'. But John knows he won't. John is thirty years of age he would like to settle down, marry and rear a family. The tractor was going to be a big help, but now that's gone. We're meeting Sunday night for the dance. He'll tell me what his plans are then. Oh! Mary I don't know what is going to happen, say a prayer for us'. 'Chin up Brid' I told her. The week went by slowly, mam and myself were sitting at the fire, the house was quiet. 'Has Brid told you about the trouble up at Kelly's? Did Brid say anything to you about it'? mum enquired. 'She did' I said. 'John and his dad are not talking since the incident about the tractor, his mam was upset, it was a terrible thing his dad has done and he the only one they have'. 'As sure as you're sitting there Mary, I tell ya John will high tail it off to England'. 'He would never do that mam, what about his mother?' 'Well Mary, the air that's going around in that house now is not good for any of them. It would be better if he did go. Worse could happen' muttered mam. Why am I recalling all these unhappy times, that happened so long ago. Is Brid sending me some sort of message, maybe like myself she is lonely. Remembering the Sunday night John and Brid were to meet, he was to divulge his plan to her at the ceilí, it sends a shiver down my spine. Pretending we weren't watching as Brid was getting ready for the ceilí, straightening the seams of her stockings, patting the powder puff around her face, the usual as she headed out the door. Mam shouted after her, 'have a good night Brid'. Remembering how happy and flushed she would be coming in after a great nights dancing.

Let Down

It wasn't to be that great a Sunday night of dancing as Brid was back in less than an hour, going straight into the bedroom. 'Go see what happened Mary, go talk to her' mam coaxing me. 'No mam, you go, please', I insisted. Going slowly into the room mam gave a look back at me, I waved my hand at her to keep going. Spending a while with Brid, coming out of the room mam was drying he eyes. 'What happened mam? Was it bad'? 'Bad Mary isn't the name for it'. 'Did John meet her'? Mam shook her head, 'no he did not come at all to meet her, and worse still he gave the message to young Tommy Burke to tell her he had gone to England. Indeed Mary he had his mind made up when they were arranging to meet for the dance to hightail it off, mark my words' mam answered. 'Do you think she will go to England after him? After all she has a nice bit of money saved away in the post office from the knitting. She was saving for her wedding day and maybe this is how it's to be. Should I go in and talk to her mam'? 'No Mary, leave her be, she has to work this out herself, it's going to take time. I doubt very much she would spend her hard earned money going after a man who didn't think enough of her to tell her face to face what he intended to do, instead he cowardly passed on it through a stranger, you can well imagine the gossip that's already ranting through the village'.

The weeks that followed was hard on mam and dad watching their oldest daughter lying in bed day after day sipping mugs of tea and eating nothing, almost fading before their very eyes.

Dad Passes Away

One morning mam called Brid, 'It's your dad Brid, he has taken bad, come there's a good girl, come and see him. He's gone Brid'. 'God have mercy on you dad', says Brid. 'John Kelly you need never show your ugly face here abouts again, look what you've done to our poor dad'. 'Hush Brid', mam tried to console, 'he had a bad heart and God called him, his time was up. Quick Mary, hop on your bike and go for Father Clancy'. I was out the door before she had finished her sentence. Riding as fast as I could to get to the Parish house. Father Clancy's housekeeper invited me into the parlour. 'Sit there' she said, 'I'll tell Father, he will be down to you in a few minutes'. Then she brought me a lovely hot cup of tea. Coming into the room Father Clancy reached out his hand, 'Mary O'Brien is it? A bit of trouble at home is there'? 'Yes Father' I said, 'Dad passed away this morning', I said between sobs.

'God rest Pat O'Brien' Father Clancy said holding his hands in prayer motion, 'I'll prepare for his mass and funeral. Call in the Doctor to sign the Death Certificate and get Joe Purcell to make ready the horse and cart to bring the coffin to St Ann's Chapel, he will only charge you a few shillings. He'll tell the grave diggers to pick a spot. Has your Mother a grave in the old Creag graveyard'?. 'No Father, we haven't', I told him. 'I'll call into my sister Nurse Clancy, she will lay him out. Has your mother the brown shroud Mary'? 'She has Father'. 'Tell her to leave it near the corpse. I'll get someone to go down to Flannery's Carpentry for the coffin. I would like to go with whoever it is. And so you can Mary, I'm on my way now to give him extremunction, the soul is with the body for three hours after the last breath is drawn, so no need to worry about that Mary'. 'Thanks Father, mam has the last rites crucifix and cloth'. 'Very good Mary. Tell your mam and Brid to ready the house for the wake, the neighbours will help you out'. Back in the house mam said she thought dad never looked so peaceful. 'He has met his maker now Mary'. Dad was very respected in the village, you could tell by the crowd that came to the wake to pay their respects. John Kelly's parents also came to the wake and shook hands with mam and me. Brid stayed outside until they left. Neighbours made sandwiches, buns and tea. The Considines sent in a barrel of stout, and the workers from the mill made a guard of honour.

    I won't ever forget the slow step of Joe Purcell's horse as he pulled the cart with dad's coffin lying across it, going down that old dirt road. The harsh rattle of the wheels tearing at my very chest with every step of the horse. Mam with Brid on one side of her and myself on the other side of her, walking slowly behind dressed in black coat and scarves borrowed from some of our good neighbours. As we reached Saint Ann's it started to rain, someone said 'happy is the corpse the rain rains on'. Father Clancy gave a lovely talk about dad, of his life, the good honest man he was. Laying him to his final resting place was hard on mam, Brid and myself held close to her. So long ago to be recalling poor dad's funeral. Going to work each morning gave me a break from the loneliness of the house. I never thought coming in sight of the old mill would cheer me up. Chatting with the work mates helped me forget for a while. Returning home in the evenings I could feel the lonely emptiness reaching out to me. Mam would try to be cheerful and ask about things that went on at the mill. I would fill her in as best I could; it helped her to forget for a while.

Brid Starts to Knit Again

A few months after dad passed away Brid brought out her knitting for the first time and in a cheerful voice she said, 'The young Maloney's had a baby boy last week, the Granny Maloney called into have a chat with mam and brought me a lovely pattern to knit a baby blanket for the cradle. I hope I'll be able to follow it. I have plenty of blue wool, Mary could you get me a couple of white hanks'? She asked handing me the money, 'I would like to put a white border on it'. 'Of course Brid I will', I told her. As I was about to sit down mam called me, 'come out and help me put in the geese'. I knew it was one of her pretences to have one of her secret chats with me. 'An answer to prayer Mary, it had to be God himself that sent in old Mrs Maloney with the knitting pattern for the baby blanket. Did you feel the black cloud lifting Mary'? 'I did mam. I think the John Kelly crisis has passed. Poor Brid she has cried enough over what happened between herself and Kelly. I think she should give knitting classes, forget about trying to run the little farm, would you mind that mam'? 'No, but I would like to keep the fowl, a cow or two and a field would be needed for them'. The plans poor mam and myself would talk about, everything looked so simple and easy as we chatted. Back to reality, we had better go in, see how Brid is getting on with the new pattern.

My First Ceílí

The excitement of my first ceílí is still with me, as I recall looking forward to it I was twenty one and all grown up. Telling Brid I would really like her to come with me. I had two reasons, one to have her company, the second I would like to see her going out to the dances again. I hoped she wouldn't refuse my request, doing all the coaxing I could think of I finally won her over. 'Did you get her to say she would go with you'? mam asked, a worried look in her eyes. 'I did mam'. Joining her hands and looking up to heaven, 'Thank you God' she prayed. Later, after agreeing to come to the ceílí, Brid went to town, coming through the kitchen she went straight to the bedroom, some parcels in her hands, mam and I looked at each other now what's up, we wondered? 'Mary', shouted Brid, 'come in a minute'. I didn't know what to expect, opening the bedroom door, I peeped in, 'what do you think of this'? Brid asked as she stood there wearing the most beautiful navy blue dress with white flowers scattered around it, a pair of navy high heeled shoes, pearl necklace and her hair styled. 'My God Brid', I said 'you look like a princess, is this for our night out I asked'? 'It is' she said, 'now you get dressed and we'll see how well we will look'. I put on my white frilled blouse, navy pleated skirt and my new navy shoes. Dancing up and down the room together, I was singing 'I'm twenty one, I can do what I like, I don't have to ask anyone'. Mam was peeping in the door, 'am I going to loose my two beautiful daughters at this ceílí', she laughed. 'You might loose one' says Brid, 'but you'll never loose this one'. 'Ah Brid', mam and I echoed, 'there's more than one fish in the sea'. 'What do you think of the neck line of my new dress, is it too low Mary'? Brid asked me. 'Not at all, the pearls show it off beautiful. You'll have all the lads racing across the floor for you, I won't get a look in'. 'I didn't say anything to ye this morning about my shopping plan. I went to the post office withdrew some of the knitting monies,' 'spend it on yourself Brid' I said, 'you've earned it'. 'And how right you are Brid'. Then the three of us hugged each other. Having changed back into our old clothes, going into the kitchen mam had laid the table and her usual currant bread was sliced and buttered on a lovely bread plate. 'This is nice mam' we told her. 'It's time to celebrate' says our mam as we sat down to eat there was a lot of reminiscing done (just as I'm doing right now).

My Twenty First

Looking back on my twenty first birthday and getting ready for my first important ceilí. All I had in mind was dance the two shoes off my feet, at the same time hoping they wouldn't cut my heels. There were some surprises in store for me. First one, Brid brought in a cake with twenty one candles lighting on it. The music played happy birthday in the background; everyone clapped their hands as I blew out the candles. Nora Murphy from The Cottage gave me a lovely scarf and wrapped it around my neck straight away. Joan Considine gave me a black silk purse. Nora and Joan were my two best friends in the woollen mill. I hugged and kissed them both for their gifts. I watched Brid; she was asked out in almost every dance, she looked so pretty twirling around the floor. On our way home we were both thinking of mam on her own, a big change now that dad was gone. On entering the kitchen mam was just finishing the Rosary, the kettle was boiling. 'I'll make a pot of tea' she said asking at the same time 'how did the night go'? 'How about the birthday cake, did it survive'? She asked Brid. 'You knew about that too'? I asked. Both mam and Brid had a good laugh at me. 'How did you get it to the hall? I asked. 'On the carrier of the bike'. 'Is that what you had? I thought it was a spare pair of shoes'. 'Did you enjoy yourself Brid?' mam asked. 'I'm glad I went' she answered. There was no more said about the dance and mam relaxed. Going into her bedroom mam brought out a little parcel, 'here, this is for you Mary, a happy birthday'. 'Not another present'? I said opening it. Inside a neat little box was a lovely blue rosary beads. 'Oh! Thanks mam' I said hugging her. 'Thank you both, this is the best birthday I have ever had'. And as I look back through the years I believe it still is. The three of us sat looking into the fire as it was slowly dying away, sipping cups of tea, each one thinking her own thoughts. 'Good night' I said, 'or is it good morning? I'm off to bed, I have work in the morning and a card to sign in on time or I'll be docked in my pay'.

Emigration Plans

Over hearing Nora and Joan discussing plans to go to America, I was filled with curiosity. Moving closer to them I said 'what is this I'm hearing'? Joan said 'how did you hear us? And we whispering, I hope no-one else here in the mill over heard us. We're thinking of emigration. You know my Uncle John, daddy's brother, has a ranch in Texas. He would sponsor us out'. 'Ranch Joan, what's a ranch'? I quizzed. 'In other words a farm' Joan replied. 'That would be alright for you Joan, you have relations there, sure Nora and I have no-one in America' I pointed out to Joan. Joan quickly replied with 'that makes no difference Mary, from once they sign the papers they're responsible for us. I'm writing to Uncle John asking him to sponsor us out, are you sure you want to emigrate too Mary'? 'I'm very sure. But Joan how about paying our way over'? 'Uncle John pays for our passage and everything Mary. Only thing he asks is we work for him for a year in return to cover his expenses. We get our room and board on the ranch'. 'A year without pay' I said, 'that seems a very long time'. 'Well Mary how long are you working in this mill'? 'About six years' I said. 'And like us, what have you after that length of time'? asked Nora. 'Nothing' I answered. 'Do you think you could put a word in for me too Joan, maybe I might have a chance too'. 'I will, but you must promise not a word about it to anyone, not even your mother or Brid. If you do we could lose our jobs'. 'I promise my lips are sealed'.

Going into bed that night the surge of excitement inside me I could hardly contain myself, never closing an eye that night, I looked across at Brid in her bed, she was sleeping sound, I think if she was awake I would have told her. Thankfully she wasn't. Then as the weeks passed I thought Joan must have forgotten all about the emigration plans. 'Well', I said to myself, 'that's that then, you're going to be stuck where you are for all eternity'.

Leaving work one evening Joan tapped me on the shoulder, 'come up to the house this evening, the papers have come. We must fill them in as soon as we can and send them away. I'll tell you about the rest this evening' Joan whispered to me. 'You gave me a shock Joan. I thought it was all forgotten. When did the papers come'? 'Yesterday'. Putting her fingers to her lips, 'mum's the word', she said. I nodded. I wondered if she felt the same surge of excitement as me. That evening I made an excuse that I was going to visit Joan for a while. Brid made sure I cleared the table after dinner and washed up. Making a remark, 'you are very great with Joan Considine'. I said 'Joan and Nora are my best friends'. I was glad to get inside Joan's door. Joan was sitting at the table, Nora opposite her, sheets of paper out in front of them. 'There's your envelope', Nora said while handing it to me. 'There are some questions in the papers you'll have to lie about, like are you related? That's a yes, what way related? Niece and so on, I'll help you if you get stuck. We have to get three passport photos each, we pay for them ourselves, a reference from the Parish Priest, and a character reference from the Garda, we don't need parent's permission as we are over twenty one'. 'Will Father Clancy say anything to Mam'? I asked Nora, in hope he wouldn't. 'Tell him you don't want it known in case you lose your job at the mill, if the Emigration Authorities turn you down, offer him a couple of shillings. I'll get the stamps and give them to you, you and Nora will have to do the rest on Saturday and post off immediately. Put my return address on yours Mary, save a lot of explaining at home. Not that we are having any secrets, but you know what a slip of the tongue could do'.

Some weeks later Nora whispered to me on the way into the mill, 'Joan got word yesterday. Next week, Tuesday and Wednesday make an excuse that we are going sight seeing in Dublin for a couple of days'. The thought of going up to Dublin to the American Embassy filled me with dread. 'Pull yourself together or you'll be in bits by next week' I told myself.

Now to tell mam and Brid as casual as I could that Joan, Nora and myself were heading to Dublin for a two day outing was a little daunting. 'Did you hear that Brid'? says mam, 'the three of them off to the big city and for two days no less'. 'Oh! Isn't it well for some', says Brid they can take off at the drop of a hat'. 'Don't mind her Mary', says mam, 'sure a couple of days sight seeing will hurt no-one. What about you Brid, why don't you go with them. A couple of days away would do you no harm'. At this suggestion from mam I thought I would wet myself, keeping my legs crossed as I stood in the middle of the kitchen floor waiting for Brid's answer, relief came as she said, 'I would go flying but I promised the Maloney's I would have the Christening shawl ready for Sunday, and I haven't even started it yet. Count me in the next time Mary'. Hurrying out the door in pretence of checking my bike was it alright for the early morning cycle to the railway station. I rushed for the shed; 'thank goodness' I said to myself, I didn't let myself down in the kitchen. Joining my hands I said 'thank heavens for the knitting'. Boy, but that was close.

Margaret Dowling

Going to Dublin

The train trip to Dublin was long and arduous. Listening to the wheels going clunk-ed-d-clunk along the line. Excitement of different feelings would rise up in our chests. 'Will we get there on time? What questions will we be asked? If we keep this up' says Joan 'we will be nervous wrecks by the time we reach the embassy'.

The big important American Council was scary to look at. There were hundreds like ourselves heading for the boat. Sitting waiting our turns to go into the daunting Consul office to be questioned. As we waited a lady came towards us in a black coat with a red rose in the lapel and her name pinned also to her coat. "I'm Mrs Grant; I'm here to take the names of those who have no accommodation for the night'. We gave our names as did many more. 'I will meet you all at the Embassy door at six pm to take you to the Convent; ye will be served tea, bread, butter and a fry. Breakfast in the morning will consist of oatmeal porridge, tea, bread and butter and the cost per head is five shillings. Ye will be called at seven am. Good luck to ye now'.

'Five shillings' says Nora, 'not bad'. Don't forget you need money for the bus', says Joan, 'how much have we? We each had twelve shillings, which should cover everything'. Going into the office, I thought its now or never, the Consul had my papers in front of him, one of the many questions I was asked was what relation is this man to you? 'My uncle', I lied. Is he married? 'Yes'. Has he a family? 'Yes, two daughters'. He has a ranch in Texas? 'Yes, Sir', I said with my voice trembling. 'You should be alright there' he said. 'You must be at the Embassy at eight in the morning. Send the next one in'. Joan was next, 'how was it'? She asked. 'Not so bad' I said, almost fainting. 'We met Mrs Grant like she said; she took us right across town in the bus'. Nora was wondering if we were safe at all. There were at least fifteen of us going to the same convent. Two nuns met us at the door. Taking us up to a dormitory where each of us had a cubicle, it was lovely and clean. The nuns said we could wash and freshen up, but regretted there was no hot water. 'Be in the dining hall at seven thirty. Rosary is eight thirty, and then to bed, you will be called at six am the following morning. Be in the dining hall six thirty for a short prayer before breakfast, ye will be at the door at seven fifteen to be taken back by Mrs Grant to the embassy. Tonight at prayer time we will take ye'er five shillings'. The sister was very nice, but very precise and clear (we were glad of the prayers).

Back at the Embassy we were now in a different department. As we lined up for the medical we were each handed a paper bag and a white coat and told to go and change in a little changing room laid out for the purpose. Sitting side by side on benches we waited our turn. Nora was sure she would be turned down because of the mole on her back. Stop worrying we told her, everyone has something wrong with them. Examiners were constantly tooing and froing. I was called in into a small cubicle, x-rayed, eyes examined, knees banged with a rubber mallet, my reflexes were alright so was my eyesight. Then questions – 'any time had I TB'?, 'no', 'any insanity in the family'?, 'no', on and on it went, every answer no. Next I had to sign a form swearing all my answers were true. 'Now you're finished, get dressed, and call at the front desk before you leave'. 'Thank you' I said and rushed off to the dressing room just as Nora was called in. Joan was there before me. I was almost dressed when Nora walked in saying 'thank heavens they said nothing about my mole'. At the front desk waiting in line for the last time we hoped. Been handed two envelopes one marked DON'T OPEN, it was for the emigration officers when we arrived in the states, 'I bet it's the x-ray' said Joan. The other one held emigration papers, passport, birth cert and other documents. We thanked God we were this far. Outside the door a group had gathered around a girl who was crying inconsolably. Nora asked someone what had happened? She said TB spots showed up in her x-ray. She was turned down and has to go into a sanatorium, when she arrives back in Cork, the poor girl. Now we really considered ourselves lucky.

Margaret Dowling

On The Train Coming Home

Boarding the train at last in Kingsbridge Station, Dublin, we were a tired but happy threesome. The carriage was a comfortable closed in unit with velvet upholstery seats, the windows opened up and down by pulling a sash. Seating ourselves comfortably and keeping our prestigious emigration documents safely by our sides. We relaxed for the first time in about three weeks. Nora as usual with a little doubt in her mind said 'she hoped it was all going to be worth it'. It was a dark and cold evening when we arrived into Limerick. Making our way to old Bridget Hogan's who kept our three bicycles for the two nights for a shilling each. 'Thanks Bridget' we said as we took hold of our bikes. 'Thanks yerselves girls, I hope ye got on well in Dublin' says she. 'Oh! We had a great time sightseeing' says Nora. 'Sightseeing indeed!' says Bridget. 'Ye look like three lassies that could afford it too, don't worry y'er secret is safe with me' she laughed.

Without another word we peddled our way slowly up the hill to home. Mam and Brid were in bed fast asleep. As usual mam had left the paraffin oil lamp on the dim light; I turned the knob to bring up the wick to get a better light. It was then the full realisation hit me, how many more times would I turn up that same little wick. I sat down and cried. Turning off the light I went to bed for I was very tired.

Sharing a Joke

The three of us were laughing and giggling in the mill, next morning one lad shouted across the wool bins, 'what's got into you three, have ye cracked y'er funny bone'? 'Oh! You'll find out soon enough' shouted Nora back. 'Have you told your mam and Brid the news yet Mary'? enquired Nora. 'It was so late when I got in last night, they were both asleep. I was glad they were for I was so tired all I could do was fall asleep. This evening now Nora, I'll give them a big surprise with my emigration news'. If I thought they were going to be surprised I was not prepared for the reception they gave me.

Recalling that evening so long ago still sends chills through me. I asked Nora if she told her Mother 'I did', said Nora. 'What did she say? Was she sad or angry'? 'Good God Mary she wasn't angry, all she said was God go with you Nora. I don't like leaving her; she will be all alone in the little cottage, poor woman. It has always been the two of us since poor dad died, may he rest in peace'. 'Did you know your dad Nora'? I asked, 'I was four years old, so I suppose I should have some little recollection of him, but there again, I don't' Nora said whilst trying to recall a memory of her dad. 'Well at least I can count on Aunt Jane calling in for a visit; she's mam's sister and likes an ould chin wag with mam. She loves gossip and she's going to have a big time with this emigration news'.

Joan's parents were aware of Joan's plans for quite some time, but you can well imagine how they were trying to ignore it having two sons already in America. The father was disappointed his oldest son Sean to leave, he was counting on him to stay on the farm and help, the land would be Sean's in the end anyway. The Considines have good land. Only the emigration bug bit both Sean and his younger brother Patsy at the same time. The two of them headed off to their Uncle Tom's ranch in Texas. 'God go with ye', said their dad. 'Joan will have great joy in meeting her two brothers and Uncle'. 'She will Mary, it's going to be lonely on her young sister Alice, herself and Joan were very great with each other, just like you and Brid. I'll see you in the morning Nora, bye for now'.

Breaking the News

Coming up the path, I could smell mam's beef stew with carrots, parsnips and onions and the lovely floury spuds. It hit me right in the nose. Mam had the table set with the bowl of lovely stew placed in the centre of the table. 'Come on girls, sit into the table, I'm sure you're good and hungry. Let's say grace, then I want to hear Mary's news and how she enjoyed sightseeing in the big city'. 'Come on' urged Brid; 'let's see the style you bought, after two days away you must have bought out the shops'?

Brid was in such a good sense of humour I had no hesitation in telling my news. 'Well' I said, 'we weren't shopping at all. It's a long story and I hope what I'm going to tell the two of ye won't come as too big a shock'. 'Listen to her', says Brid, 'I bet she got herself a job in the Big City, fed up with the woollen mill'. 'Ah!' says mam, 'who can blame her, they don't get paid enough at all there and the long hours they work'. 'No' I said, 'that's not it at all'. As my story unfolded about emigration, the help I got from Joan Considine with the paper, the filling in of forms. How her Uncle Sean in Texas who was the owner of a big ranch there would be claiming us out and giving us work as I tried to make the news as simple and easy as I could. I was not ready for what came next in that little kitchen, coming to my mind so vivid can still tear at my heart. I hadn't finished all I had to tell. When the crash of a chair frightened me, as Brid sprang to her feet and coming down on the table with a crash of her fist sending mam's bowl of stew to the rafters. 'My God' she roared, 'them Considine's should be hunted out of the parish of Ballygala. They're enticing all the young people away to this great ranch of their uncles' in Texas. As for that cocky Joan, I never did like her. But you Mary, you follow her around like a puppy dog'.

Well, if I thought them words were harsh, what she said next threw me entirely. 'You Mary O'Brien heading out to America soon from what you're saying, you needn't wait until then, but gather your things and your famous 'visa' and get out of this house this very evening and sleep with them Considines. I don't want to see your sly face here abouts again', giving the table another rap of her fist.

Shaking to my very roots on hearing such hard words coming from the lips of my only sister. But if that shocked me, what happened next and coming from mam, who was always a quiet and docile woman even poor dad never uttered a cross word to his two daughters, may they both Rest in Peace at this time.

Mam Makes a Stand

Mam standing up to her full height of five foot and slight frame, looking at Brid and in a low fierce tone she said, 'I'm still the owner of this house, and I'll say who goes and who stays. There's one question I want you to answer Mary, why didn't you tell us sooner what you were planning'? 'I couldn't mam, if it was found out at the mill we were going to emigrate, we would lose our jobs there and then, and if the emigration authorities turned us down we would be at a loss, and I promised Joan I wouldn't say a word even though it was hard not too'. 'Joan, so you promised Joan', Brid shot at me. 'I knew she was at the back of it'. 'Yes', I said, 'I did promise her, and now I'm very glad I did, seeing your outburst'. 'Well' she says, 'you're not gone yet'. Turning and pointing a finger at mam, 'don't you write that letter giving her your permission, if you do you're worse than she is' a cross Brid said. 'One minute Brid, I don't need permission from mam; all I want from her is her blessing. I'm twenty one years of age; I'm old enough to know what I want'. 'Sure you're twenty one, you know it all. Why wouldn't you, you got the schooling, you're the educated one' Brid threw back to me. Mam still standing took a look at Brid; 'if that's a dig at me you can take it back this minute Brid. Trying to get you out of your bed in the mornings was a hardship on me. Your poor dad, may he rest in peace, would say to me leave her there, sure devil a much schooling we got ourselves and aren't we doing alright. The mornings I did get you up I had to bribe you. Your sister there was telling lies to the teacher covering up for you, saying how sick you were. And myself lying to the teacher if I met her after Mass. Is Brid delicate? Did you get a doctors opinion? Get her a tonic Mrs O'Brien. I will I'd lie'. 'Indeed mam you were well able to dish out the work to me. Let Mary sit down she has her lessons to do'. 'Yes, she had her lessons to do, and she walked the two miles to and from school day in day out, wet or dry, while you lay on in the bed' mam said defending me. 'Well Brid you domineered me then and I'll admit I needed your help when Mary was born, I had to depend on you, you were a good little worker even at eight years old. Well it's all in the past and I'm not letting anyone domineer me in my own house again'. I never knew mam had trouble from Brid but then I was young and out at school. Poor mam had it hard. 'Now Mary, when are ye taking the boat'? Mam asked. 'Six weeks from now, I'll work for five and give in my notice. The last week I'll need to buy a few things, suitcase, towel, soap, things I'll need on the ship. They gave us a list when we were in Dublin'. 'Six weeks you say, well Mary, you're welcome to stay in your mothers' and sisters' house until then and you're always welcome back. There's one thing I want from the two of ye this evening, it's to shake hands and make up; we'll put all of this behind us. I certainly don't want the atmosphere in this house like what went on in Kelly's. Poor Mrs Kelly was here for a visit last week and told me all about what she had to endure. She tells me the ould man is in failing health and not a word will he return to his only son John, tears in her eyes. Even when John asked us over to his wedding, he sent the tickets for us to go; I had to send them back to him. I wouldn't be able to travel that distance on my own, she told me. He understood how it was for me, and with a laugh she says, he married an English girl, I never said it to his ould fellow'.

Out of the blue Brid asks 'did she say anything about me'? 'Mrs Kelly regrets that terrible morning', she says 'I would have loved to have Brid O'Brien in my kitchen. I was glad of her visit and to know there's no bitterness between us', says mam. 'What kind of work is John at in England mam', I asked? 'He is at the building and his wife is head Sister in a hospital'. 'There you are', says Brid; 'I wouldn't have been good enough for him at all'. 'Hold your tongue Brid' says mam; 'you have all that well put behind you now'.

A Solution

'**N**ow I'm going to suggest Mary you take your belongings and put them in my room, use it while you're here, you'll be able to do your packing in comfort, and anyway you would only be getting in Brid's way, and I'll sleep in your bed, in Brid's room, now won't that suit'?.

'Thanks mam' I said going into the room I shared with Brid for over twenty years. I thought, Thank God we're friends again, poor mam, she was a peace maker. As I went to get my things Brid had come into the room behind me. I turned to give her a smile, the look of hatred in her eyes almost struck me dead. Mam stuck her head in the door as Brid went and sat on the side of her bed. 'I forgot to ask you Mary, how are you travelling to Queens Town for the boat'? 'The Considine's are hiring a hackney' I answered. 'And how much will it cost you Mary? 'No charge', and then I explained how we would work a year without wages as repayment to cover the Considine's expenses. 'We will have room and board on the ranch. When the year is up they will start to pay us'. 'I have you tormented Mary with questions', says mam. 'What kind of work will you be doing on the American Farm'? 'I don't know yet mam' 'and will you have a room to yourself'? Before I could answer, Brid cut in, 'don't you know Joan will have an office job and didn't she get a taste of it in the mill when the pay mistress was out sick, and you know very well when it's her uncles ranch (we must say ranch) she'll have her own bedroom and sleeping between silk sheets, as for you Mary, and Nora from the cottage, ye'll be slopping out the pigs and sleeping with them'. At that remark mam let out a big hearty laugh. 'Brid' she says, 'its St Patrick you're thinking about'. It was good to hear mam laugh. 'When will you hand in your notice Mary'? 'Three weeks time, give two weeks notice and a week at home to prepare to leave'. 'When you have five weeks to work and make a little money keep it for the things you said you need to buy, you have handed in enough money to this house' mam replied.

'No mam, I couldn't do that, I'll keep the last weeks wages that should get me what I need. Thanks very much and as I apologised for any trouble I might have caused'. I could see the smirk on Brid's face. 'You didn't intend to cause trouble Mary, now I'll go and make some toast and scrambled eggs, would ye like that'? We both nodded our heads. As I gathered up my belongings which wasn't much and leaving the room I could hear Brid mumble, 'be sure it's only your own you're taking'.

Laying my stuff on dad and mam's bed, I thought how right it was to be using their room, my last weeks in the house.

American Wake

I remember saying 'mam no American Wake for me, it wouldn't be fair on our poor neighbours especially as there's three of us going at the one time'. 'I know you're right Mary, but a little get together up in the hall would be nice, ye'r last Sunday night here. I'll have a word with Nora's mother after Mass on Sunday. We could have some tea with cake and maybe an olde sing song'.

As we sat at the table eating mam's delicious scrambled eggs, mam kept up her chat about emigration and her young daughter taking the boat. I knew by Brid's restlessness she would just as soon leave the table, but she had to keep up the pretence of friendship with me; the next six weeks would be long for her too. No one mentioned the stew; mam had cleared away the mess. 'Well mam' I said, 'seeing as you put it that way, it's probably a good idea'. No sooner were the words out of my mouth than Brid says, 'mam I won't be there'. 'Why not Brid? It will be a little farewell for your sister and friends. You will come Brid, why wouldn't you'? 'Look around you at the amount of knitting I'm facing and work I've promised to have ready weeks ago'. Mam's face was red, 'it won't be the same without you, and anyway I've never yet seen you knitting on a Sunday'.

Going into work next morning, I felt as if a train had hit me. Nora walked over to me from her work bench. 'Mary you look like hell, it didn't go too well did it'? 'Oh Nora! Brid hit the roof, she called me sly, I can't tell you the half of it'. 'And your mam, how did she take the news'? Nora enquired. 'Not too bad, she thought I should have told them about my plans first (I'm lucky I didn't), in fact she's talking about meeting your mother to make plans for a ceílí for our last Sunday night here'. 'Great, my mother will be all for that. So things are bad between you and Brid'? 'Yes and six weeks is a long time to live in pretence, but I'm doing it for poor mam's sake'.

Hiding the Visa

'**W**hat have you in the bag Mary'? 'To tell you the truth Nora, I couldn't trust Brid to leave my passport and emigration papers in the house so I brought them to work with me'. 'Mary dear, you poor thing, here I'll get Joan to look after them for you'. 'Thanks Nora, I don't know what I would do without yourself and Joan'. Brid has lots of friends especially through the knitting. Looking back she had a lot more friends than me. I never criticise any of them. Maggie Conroy was always coming to the house to talk to Brid and hold the hanks of wool for Brid to roll it into balls. Brid would give Maggie a few shillings for her help as Maggie would say 'for the smokes'. Poor Maggie was born with a short leg and was unable to go out to work so this little job came in very handy for her. The tension between Brid and myself and the nasty digs she would give me at every opportunity. I was afraid mam would notice and be upset. I was enjoying watching her busy baking her buns and cakes for the American wake, taking out a dress she hadn't worn in a long time, looking at it she says 'I wonder will it fit me after all these years, its been lying in the wardrobe, it's a wonder the moths haven't eaten it'.

A Visit to Father Clancy

Calling and having a chat with Father Clancy I hoped would clear my head and help me feel better before departing. I knocked on his door, he answered it himself. 'Hello Mary, you're very welcome', showing me into the parlour. 'Sit by the fire there Mary, I believe you're taking the boat'. We both laughed. 'Bridget will bring us tea and some of her apple tart'. Sitting by his cosy fire loosened my tongue. I told him my troubles and the anger Brid was in, and we faking peace between us for mam's sake. 'I'll be glad to get away from Brid Father'. 'Don't be too hard on your sister Mary, she's how she is, and can't help it. It was hard on her when John Kelly left the way he did; it was a big blow to her. As for her schooling, no matter what your mother says it suited her to have Brid at home helping her. I'm going to let you in on something private and keep it to yourself, telling you this might be a help and maybe you'll understand your family better. Your dad, may he rest in peace, knew for years he had a bad heart and that was the reason they came to me, it's a long time ago, he wanted help making his will, leaving all to Brid'.

The Will

'Well' I said, as the blood rushed to my face, how many more shocks will I get before I leave Ballygala'? 'Listen to me Mary, aren't you doing what is right for yourself. That little home place sure there's not enough in it to share with a cat. Brid is lucky to have her knitting talent; she will be able to save a bit of money for herself. God is good, she'll get herself a nice man yet to settle down with. Your poor mother is trying to make it up to you. You're the one who has kept the food on the table since ever you started working in the woollen mill. Your dad, may he rest in peace, made the right move and hasn't this proved it. Now Mary, if ever you want any news of home or anything, just write to me and I'll be here to answer your letters. Not a word about the will, promise me'. 'I promise', I said. Giving me his blessing, and saying 'I'll see you Sunday night at the American Wake'.

I left his house feeling much better in myself and with a better feeling for my family than I thought possible. That was one of a couple of important items on my list I had to do, which I hadn't mentioned to mam. Next important duty, visit dad's grave with a little shovel and a few primrose roots. I made a little flower bed. Asking his forgiveness for any wrong done, and telling him Brid and myself were not talking; I pray we make up before I leave. Kissing the ground I said my last goodbye. Shedding tears I said 'dad you knew what you were doing when you made the will'.

Margaret Dowling

Last Good Bye's

That Sunday night I had a mixture of joy and sorrow. The hall tables were set, mam's baking stood out, Nora's mother made sandwiches, other neighbours made tea, Considine's hired music. The lads from the mill brought the drink. The ceílí was at its best, everyone enjoying themselves. Looking at mam in her lovely dress with white lace collar, she was I thought, once a beauty no doubt. The lads danced the feet off us that night, rushing the three emigrant lassies to the floor for every set. Soon it was hush time, the music stopped. Tom Considine introduced Father Clancy, saying 'our Parish Priest would like to say a few words to ye now, and on behalf of the three girls I wish to thank everyone who made it so enjoyable in spite of the sadness, now it's over to you Father'. 'Thank you. I won't keep ye long, what I have to say is convey to ye my deep regrets at the drain of youth from this Parish, how our young people are fast leaving us. Three of our young girls taking the boat tomorrow to seek their fortune further afield. It's a great loss of trained workers from our mill, and sad to say, the birth of new babies to increase the population is few and far between. But however, in this year of 1937, we wish the three lovely lassies a safe and happy life in the Texas prairie'. Everyone clapped and began shouting 'don't forget to send home the dollars and the parcels!' Before the night finished Mickey the village joker shouted 't'was a great night', everyone cheered again. 'We should have more American Wakes'. A woman beat him out the door with a tea towel, and everyone roared laughing. The times back in the thirty's was hard, but we always had something to laugh at. Joan and Nora came over to me. 'Brid never showed her face at all' they both said together. 'I know' I said, 'I watched the door all night'. 'Never mind, well we'll see you at five in the morning'. The hackney cab was right on time. Mam was coming with me. Mrs Murphy was with Nora, Joan's younger sister Alice came with her, her mam and dad said they had seen two of their family board a ship already, they didn't want to see a third.

Sad Partings

Passing my house for the last time Brid was standing at the door in a beautiful hand knitted dressing gown. 'Oh!' says Alice, 'isn't Brid's dressing gown beautiful'. 'Yes' says mam, all her own hand work. 'Would she knit one for me Mrs O'Brien'? Alice asked. 'Indeed she would Alice, just tell her what you want, it would keep her busy; keep her from being lonely after Mary'. Nora gave me a nudge. Reliving how I tried to make friends with Brid before I left that morning. 'For one last time Brid, can't we make up', I begged. 'As long as I live I want nothing to do with you, don't attempt to come back here. If I hear of you coming I'll leave mam and I'll never set foot here again, that's my goodbye to you Mary O'Brien, my curse goes with you'. It was a cruel and sad parting. Who would ever think that Brid could turn with such hatred in her heart on her only sister? I felt a heavy hand on my heart that day; I hoped to feel better as the hackney slowly moved down the lonely road.

Arriving in Queens Town

In one sense we were glad to have arrived in Queens Town and sad at the same time. The parting was tearing the hearts out of our very chests. As for me, I knew I would never set foot in Ballygala again. Mam with her arms around me asked 'did I say goodbye to Brid'. 'I tried mam'. 'I know you did Mary and the pretence ye kept up for the past six weeks was an endurance of your love for me'. 'Mam' I said, 'you're the sly one, you knew all the time'. Our last farewells said. We headed onto the tender to take us out to the ship, the old Franconia, none of us looked back. The tender was packed with young people like ourselves leaving the ould sod, and many visitors returning after their Irish holiday. None of us felt like talking, only Nora with her sense of humour and trying to sit on a rickety wooden bench, says out loud, 'I hope they have something better than this to sit on in the ship'. This brought a laugh from those within hearing distance. At last we're ready to board the ship.

Nora Shortens the Time

Awaiting our turn to board ship, which would have seemed to take hours as most of the visitors were allowed to embark first. The rocking of the tender slowed the progress. Standing staring into space Nora appeared very preoccupied with her thoughts. With a nudge to me Joan says 'Nora seems to be in dreamland', 'Nora' we asked 'what thoughts are in your head this time'. Nora replied with 'I'm thinking' she says 'how lucky we are compared to the poor creatures who emigrated less than ten years ago'. 'Why is that Nora'? I asked. 'We don't have to go through the torture of disinfecting'. 'Nora'? we asked, 'what have you been reading'? 'I wasn't reading anything. Mam was telling me about it, she met Mrs Crowe at the market and conversation came around to me emigrating. Mrs Crowe told mam that her sister went out to America in the 1920's. There were these big vats of hot water with the smell of Jeyes Fluid steaming up out of them and they had to step into them and sit down and splash all over themselves, then step out for cold water to be thrown on them, this was meant for them not to catch cold. Next in a small cubicle a few of them together getting dressed as they shivered. Picking up their little bags they were shown to another room where attendants were waiting with big toothed racks (combs) to go through their hair'. 'Good God Nora what did they do if there were things in the hair'? we both asked. 'It was cut off and smelly type of gel was rubbed on the scalp' said Nora. 'Oh what awful treatment. Thank goodness that's stopped, if it was happening today I'd hate to think what would happen to my bushy hair' says Mary pointing to her red mop. 'Or my black mop' chimed in Nora. 'It must have been a slow job Nora'? 'Mrs Crowe said it took about an hour and a half to get through a hundred people, then again it was only for the emigrants, I don't think there was too many visitors' said Nora. 'Well Nora, you have done it again'. 'Done what? asked Nora. 'Shortened the time with that information from the past'.

A Stewart was shouting 'returning visitors this way, immigrants this side'. 'Did you hear' that says Joan, 'now we're immigrants'. We were shown to our cabin. 'Cabin' says Nora, 'the cows sleep in cabins in our village'. Some folk shot her dirty looks, while others gave half a smile. Inside the cabins was a small dark space with two sets of bunk beds. Nora was first to grab a top one 'in case' as she said, 'the sea should come in, I would be safe'. There was a little hand basin in a corner and a few hooks on the back of the door, which would serve as our wardrobe. We were joined by another girl. 'Welcome' says Nora to the cell. 'You'll need to put a zip on that mouth of yours', Joan told her, 'or you'll get us into trouble before this trip is over'. Introducing ourselves to Patricia from Mayo, the four of us shared the small cabin as best we could.

Exploring the Liner

'Let's take a stroll out on the deck' suggested Joan, of course I was afraid of getting lost. 'We won't' says Joan, 'this is our cabin number, twenty three, and we're on D deck'. 'Will you join us Patricia'? We asked. 'Thank you so much' says Patricia, 'I've a few friends in another cabin up on B deck, I'll go up to them, I'll see ye later'. As we headed up, stairs after stairs to get to the top deck, 'my God' says Nora, 'its hard work and the ship isn't sailing at all yet'. Reaching one deck that had shops we stood to look at the jewellery on the window. I will never forget the nice couple who began to talk to us. 'I'm Tom and this is my wife Betty', they were returning to Texas after their Irish holiday in Cork. 'Well what do ye think of the ship'? Tom asked. 'It's enormous', babbled Nora. 'You might think that', he answered, 'as ye'er only greenhorns yet', he smiled, a big smile flashing a large set of the whitest teeth we ever seen. 'Greenhorns'? says Joan, 'what do you mean'? Betty his wife chipped in, 'it's a nicer title than the immigrant one. Twenty years ago when we emigrated we were nicknamed greenhorns too and it's said ever since for the new inexperience travellers'. 'I think I'll like it' I said.

'We're going to get lost on this big ship' a worried Nora said. 'Big ship' says Tom, 'you think this is a big ship? You should travel on the Queen Mary sometime, now that's a liner, the biggest one in the world'. We wanted to hear more about this liner. 'Yes' says Tom, 'up to seventeen decks, a theatre, library, about ten restaurants and swimming pools.' 'Not to mention the number of passengers aboard' says Betty, 'over two and a half thousand passengers'. We were in awe at all this information. 'What about the one we're travelling on, is it a liner'? asked Joan. Tom laughed, 'no comparison, but a liner it is, maybe ten decks, some shops, six restaurants, and the food is excellent. My wife and I have sailed in her before'. 'Look at the handsome sailors', whispered Nora, 'in their navy and white'. I look back now and remember how Tom the nice gentleman smiled at her saying 'you have an eye for a sailor then'? 'No, No' says poor Nora. 'I'm just admiring their uniforms'. 'You see the big men in navy and white suits, well there the stewards, note the stripes on their sleeves, that's to distinguish the importance of their office on ship. There's two men wearing white uniforms, one is the Admiral or Ships Captain, you'll notice all his distinguishing stripes, the other man is his First Mate'. As the two men were passing they each tipped their hats to us. 'Oh! What elegance', Joan whispered. Tom and Betty said bye for a while, 'we won't see you in the dining room, for we're travelling first class, we will be watching out for you all'. 'So much information' says I, 'we will never remember it all'. 'We'll have to watch out for sleeves' quipped Nora.

As we strolled around the deck we came across a notice board giving information on what entertainment was on, the films mostly western, a concert another night, then a fancy dress afternoon. 'We don't have anything to wear at a fancy dress afternoon' Nora complained. 'We can go and see', chimed in Joan. 'Look at all the lovely chocolate bars and us not having the price of even one bar between us' I whined. 'We'll be getting our meals anyway' says Nora 'and Tom said the food is good. 'Who knows, maybe a handsome sailor will serve us. Wouldn't it be great to have one each for the ten days'? 'Yes, entertaining us', smiled Nora.

Up on top deck looking out at the view and listening to the splash, splash of the water off the side of the ship it was so peaceful, when suddenly the ship gave a heave. Then we heard shouts of 'anchors away'. Now the ship was at last moving out to sea. Unsteady on our feet we decided to go down to our cabin by the time we reached the door we were feeling very sick. Thoughts of having ten days of fun were fast disappearing from our minds. Seasickness was to be our lot, especially as we were travelling in the winter time and the sea was sure to be rough.

Advice from a head steward with three stripes on his sleeve told us, 'if you are experiencing seasickness do not remain in your cabin, go to the dining room, take some food in small amounts, protection for your stomach'. 'Oh dear', moaned Nora, 'leave our cabin, I'd just as soon stay in it until we arrive in America, I am so sick I can hardly lift my poor head'. 'I suppose we're all in the same boat. Leave it to you Nora to see the funny side'; I said giving her a hug.

We did as we were told and went to the dining room. People were seated at the tables with big plates of delicious food before them. 'Look at them people' says Nora, 'how can they muck into so much'? 'They're seasoned travellers' I whispered. How did I have such information? Sitting into the table we ordered tea and toast. No sooner had we eaten it, than we had to hurry from the table, head for the deck to throw up over the rail and that was our travelling enjoyment for most of the voyage.

Feeling the sea becoming calmer and the seasickness too was beginning to ease off. Thinking to myself we must be very near 'Port Isabel'. Now in answer to my thoughts the ship gave two big bumps as the sailors lowered the anchor. A big shout went up, everyone clapped their hands, and 'we have arrived, its Port Isabel, Texas'. Once more we were experiencing bouts of nervousness, as I remember that journey, my stomach starts to feel a bit queasy, while I sit here in my comfortable kitchen, so much has happened and changed since that time so long ago.

Joan was the first to say 'better make sure we have all our papers at the ready'. The American Consuls are boarding ship now to check us out; it was hard to take it all in. First there was ten days of wicked seasickness, now as we stand in a long line waiting for more questioning. Needless to say we were once again experiencing bouts of nervousness, which was how it was back in them years. I can remember it all like as if it was yesterday, so much has changed since then, even for me. Joan was on the ball, 'hurry, we'll need to pack up our few things, have our papers, passports and visas at the ready, the American Consuls are boarding ship now to check us out'. It was hard work taking it all in after the ten days of seasickness. We had to find our immigration line to stand in, the long line of about a thousand immigrants to be checked out for what seemed like hours, to reach the Consul who was dressed in very official uniform, no mistaking him bearing the American Emigration Official badge on his sleeve. We got through it all. Half of the time we didn't know what was taking place, the descriptive word of greenhorns fitted us alright. We were sad to say goodbye to the liner the 'Franconia'.

Disembarking

'We've arrived girls, we've arrived', Joan's enthusiasm was rubbing off on Nora and myself. Meeting her uncle was to be the next bit of excitement. 'Look at our card girls' she says. 'I have the name Considine in big print, for Uncle Tom to see, just in case he doesn't recognise me among this crowd. My two brothers will be at the ranch'. We stood what seemed like hours in the waiting hall, with thousands of others waiting to be collected, possibly by some total stranger. We were lucky to have Joan's Uncle Tom, at least he was family. Then a big man in a cowboy outfit came towards us. With a real Texan drawl 'Considine'? he asks. 'Yes' says Joan, looking bewildered. Taking a piece of paper from his pocket he read out our names and details. 'That's us' says Joan, 'where is my Uncle Tom'? 'Mr Considine is away on business Ma'am, he sent me to collect you all, and the name is Zac'. Joan was sure her uncle would be there to welcome her with open arms, her eyes filled up with tears. 'You gals hungry'? Mr Considine said 'I must take you all for food. It's a long way to the Buckboard Ranch'. Picking up our little suitcases we trailed along behind this big man as he took long striding steps in his fancy cowboy boots. 'When I get my first pay packet I'm buying myself a pair of cowboy boots' whispered Joan, in betweens sobs.

First Texan Meal

Taking us into a large restaurant Zac said 'we'll sit here, the waitress will come to serve us in a little while'. So busy was this place with all these tall Texans passing in with big plates of food in their hands. Men and women both dressed in Texan gear and talking in loud Texan drawl. Even the waitress wore the big hat as well as the boots, plaid shirt, with a short little waist coat over it, studded with sequins. The only thing to identify her as a waitress was a little check apron tied over her pants.

Dear God I thought, I'll never be able to get used to this kind of life. Coming to our table the waitress asked 'what can I get you all'? The three of us looked at each other. Zac (whom we took too, for his kindness and help) said 'you all like beef', 'yes we chorused, 'three beef sandwiches please'.

Returning with three full platters of beef, gravy and thick slices of bread, the waitress placed them in front of us. 'Oh!' We said, we only ordered sandwiches, not dinner. Zac looking at our amazed faces said 'eat up you all, you need some beef on them there bones'. 'So much beef' says Nora 'we wouldn't get that much in a year back home'. 'This is the great state of Texas' smiled Zac 'and steer is always on the menu'. 'Steer' whispered Nora 'another name for the poor cow'. 'Something to drink'? asked the waitress. 'Yes, tea please' said Joan. The waitress arrived with three tall glasses of water the colour of tea, with ice rattling in them, and a wedge of lemon on the top. Zac again to the rescue said 'Ice Tea gals, good for the thirst'.

Joan and I looked at each other hoping at the same time Nora wouldn't say out loud what we were thinking as we eyed the colour of the ice tea. 'Use the straw gals' said Zac, 'you'll enjoy it better'. Well we did and like a thousand other things we got used to it. 'You all ready now? We'll take the long drive to the Buckboard Ranch'.

Reflecting back on the many changes that took place in our young lives, where we had to acclimatise ourselves to a whole new world. It brings a tear as well as a smile. I think of Nora, of the Cottage; her sense of humour; and her definition of things you never knew what next to expect from her. Her company kept us happy as we pretended to check her when she came out with some unexpected remark in a public place where our faces would turn pure red. But again, them days are well and truly gone by now.

Accommodation

Arriving at our accommodation, stepping down from the truck, as they referred to it here, it was a comfortable, stylish lorry, seats so well cushioned. The three of us slept the long journey to the Buckboard Ranch. As we tried to walk to the building, which we would call our home for the next year or more. Our legs kept buckling under us, 'motion sickness' said Zac. 'What's that'? I asked. 'You're feeling the effects of your long voyage across the Atlantic and the fact you all suffered seasickness'. 'Dear God' says Joan, 'first seasickness, now motion sickness, what other type of sickness will we experience'? Under her breath we could hear Nora saying 'morning sickness'! Joan gave her a push asking at the same time 'will the motion sickness last long'? 'It should pass in a few days' replied Zac, as he walked us to the large building where he handed us a key. 'In you go, make yourselves at home' ushering us into the room. We thanked him and Joan unlocked the door, stepping into a huge room with five beds. 'My', said Nora, 'this is big'! 'Look' she said, 'five beds, I wonder who we're sharing with'? The room was nicely furnished with presses, a dressing table each, arm chairs, an ice box for cold drinks. Off this room was a bathroom with toilets, showers and a big bath tub. 'We'll never learn how to use them things on the wall' says Nora, pointing to the showers.

Two nice girls came in soon after us. 'Hi' said one 'I'm Livia and this is Janice'. We introduced ourselves. Then Livia said 'you change, take shower and we take you all to the dining hall for meal'. There were three showers; the two girls showed us how to use them. Nora with a laugh said 'no-one had to show us back home how to work a shower; it came straight down from the heavens'.

Taking us to the dining quarters we shared their table. The place was packed with ranch hands. 'What you want to eat'? We went for potatoes, carrots and chicken, the Italian girls picked long stringy things, Nora asked after dinner 'what had the Italian girls on their plates, were they some kind of worms'? In time we learned the Italians liked spaghetti and meatballs. It was a good start but very strange. The bed was very welcome indeed and as I lay down sleep came instantly, but oh! The dreams, my mother, I could see her away in the distance. I was rocking around in a small open boat feeling very lost. Father Clancy was far off waving to me. Waking up I was covered in sweat. 'It was only a dream' I said out loud. 'You too', said Joan from the bed next to me. 'Where is Livia and Janice'? 'They must be at work already, it's only six in the morning' says Nora 'after our journey they will probably leave us a couple of hours more'. Just then there was a rap on the door. In strode a smartly dressed woman in shorts and blouse. 'You all get up now, dress in these overalls and go to the dining hall for breakfast. Jud will be in at seven to show you your duties, now you have one hour, get moving'. Then she was gone. 'More uniforms', says Nora, 'but these are all one piece with legs and all in them'. As I put on the overalls, I wondered what Mam would say if she seen me in mans trousers. 'God forgive you Mary, wearing such things', would be her comment. The yard hand, a big burly man brought us out to the yard where he handed each of us a dung fork, 'the name's Jud' he told us, 'I look after the horse stables. I'll take you first; show you where you are going to fork out the horse dung'. Taking me to a row of stables 'this is where you will work', looking at the number of stables that stretched out in front of me it looked like about forty, turning to him I said 'how many must I do'? 'You have only to clear from the corners the manure removers are too big to reach in, now carry on'. 'Thanks' I said. Standing there with gumboots to my knees, I wished I was back in O'Flynns Woollen Mills.

After three weeks working in that job I was ready to drop dead, one evening Jud came to check on me. 'You're not doing a good job there', catching my two arms he said 'you need to build a bit of muscle'. 'Yes' I said, 'and I need a new back'. 'Oh! back trouble too. Go to your room and I'll have the nurse look in on you. You'll need a back rub'. Joan was already stretched on the bed.

The Rub Down

Nora came in the door, bent in two 'give me mill work any day' she wailed. 'Did that cowhand called Jud tell ye to come in for the nurse to have a look at ye too'? 'He did'. 'I wonder' she says 'why he was wearing two aprons, one on each leg flapping as he walked'. 'Nora, they are called chaps, cowboys and ranch hands wear them to save their jeans and legs from getting torn up with the rough shrub'. 'Thanks Joan, I learn a little every day'.

A big hefty woman, tanned copper brown, came pounding into the room, wearing shorts and sleeveless sweat shirt. 'You all the three Irish gals that failed your first work test'? She drawled. We stared, mouths open, all thinking the same thing, failed, they'll send us back. Then she laughed 'strip off, shower, don't dry, come out bare, lie belly down on your beds and I'll rub in the goose grease. Come on gals, what are ye hiding'? Embarrassing wasn't the word, we wouldn't strip in front of our mothers. Squeezing the goo onto my back she rubbed and rubbed until I thought I hadn't an inch of skin left on my back, going to each one in turns, moans and groans were coming from us as she went back and forth to each one of us.

As quickly as she started, she finished. 'You all stay here until dinner time, have a good rest. After dinner Mrs Fulton, our domestic supervisor, will interview you all for your new assignments'. We thanked her as she left. Laughing at the thought of being so naked in company, Nora said 'well the nurse didn't seem to take much notice. I hope our next assignments are easier than forking out dung. You heard her say domestic. I bet we will be all washing up dishes'. 'Lets talk no more' says Joan, 'you heard what she said, rest'. Pulling the sheets over us we went into a deep sleep. It was Livia who woke us up, 'get dressed we will go for dinner'.

New Positions

The next thought was what is Mrs Fulton like? Livia told us herself and Janice worked at peeling vegetables, but it was done by machine, telling us they were working at the Buckboard ranch two years since they came from Italy. After dinner a short stout woman came to our table, 'you three follow me to my office'. Two chairs were outside her office door, 'sit there' she told Joan and Nora. 'You, come with me'. I was quite nervous of this stern lady. 'Sit there' she told me as she went to the other side of her big desk. One question was all she asked me, 'how much education did I get'? saying I had a primary education and went as far as sixth glass. 'Very good Mary' she said, 'I will ring for Eva our head laundress, she'll show you what to do there, that's your new assignment'. Just in an instant that was done. Passing Joan in the doorway I wondered what her assignment would be, office work I thought. Eva took me to the biggest laundry room I'm sure in the world. Although late in the evening there was still people working at top speed, one laundress with a large presser was pressing sheets so fast it scared me. I hoped I wouldn't be asked to work on that. Eva spent hours showing me what my job would be, in the morning you must be here at half past six, we don't tolerate lateness. 'Good night now Mary'. Reaching my room and looking at the clock it was just twelve midnight. God I'm tired. I wondered where Joan and Nora were. I was glad I woke early next morning. Nora and Joan were asleep; I wondered should I wake them up. Tapping Joan on the shoulder I said 'It's six o'clock, what time have you to be at work'? 'Seven' she said, 'thanks'. Taking a quick breakfast I hurried to the laundry room. I set to work on tons of dirty cloths. The hum of the machines large and small drying and washing reminded me of the mill wheel and gushing water at the woollen mill. Indeed I said to myself it's a far cry from mam's washboard and the heating of the iron in the fire, she could turn out dads old shirt for Sundays Mass like a new one.

A Good Cry

Were they putting us to a test assigning us to stable work, forking out manure, sure to look at us it's obvious we wouldn't be able to clean out a hen house? We laughed at the very idea of it. Asking Joan how her meeting went with her brothers and uncle John. Immediately as I asked the question, Joan became overwhelmed with sadness and loneliness, Nora and myself were overcome with the same sad feeling. For the first time since we arrived in Texas we cried as if our hearts would break each one recalling our own sorrow. Joan remembering her great disappointment at the boat, when her uncle John failed to be there to greet her. Nora thinking of her mother left on her own in the cottage, as for me the rift with my sister Brid left a gaping wound in my heart. Our thoughts went back to the very day the papers arrived in the post in three bulky envelopes preparing us for the first leg towards emigration, and all that happened up to this very moment leaving us quite shook up. Poor Nora as usual trying to cheer us up said 'come on lets clear our heads, dry our eyes'. Joan wondered if there was anything in the ice box to help. Taking out a bottle of Tom Collins, 'come on get out the glasses, let's drink to our by-gones'.

Discussing the New Positions

Meeting for the first time in three months the three of us had so much to tell about our new jobs. 'I like working in the laundry and what I feared in the first days gals, as I watched the girl pressing the sheets and going at such a speed, well guess what I'm doing - that job now'. Nora loved the nursery work 'I'm promised permanent work in it, I'm so good with the children, they are all ages and sizes' she told us.

'How about you Joan?' we asked 'you got the grandest job using pen and paper. The education has paid off well for you'. 'I will agree it is a help for you need to know the names of all the goods and prices, have it all in order for the Chief Grocery Shopper Stephen O'Hara, he has a North of Ireland accent, he comes in a few times a week to collect it. The one thing I never order is meat; they kill and cure their own beef. There's barrels of steer meat out in the ice house. I got a look in once when a butcher was taking in a bag of salt to cure the meat. So much cuts of steak, t-bone, porter house, minute steak, prime steak, I could go on for hours. I like the pantry work; I can listen to the radio all day'. 'Sure they do the same thing with the pigs when they kill them back home', says Nora. 'How do you mean'? I asked her. 'You know, barrel then to the Ice House'. 'Oh! Nora, The Ice House, back home, ice only comes in the winter time, with the snow. I miss seeing flitchs of bacon hanging along the kitchen rafters. There was nothing to equal a slice of it boiled with turnip'. 'Oh! Stop Nora, you're making us drool'. Such was our conversations whenever we would meet up, the long hours working and different times, to relax. Late nights finishing gave us only enough time to shower and how good it felt after the steamy laundry room. Then bed and God's gift of sleep and dream of home. There were times I felt the year long before our first pay envelope. I had different plans for it. Thinking back to them days I guess you might say it was an experiencing time, I have no regrets. I would whisper to myself.

Ranch Owners

In one of our rare get togethers I asked Joan how her uncle John became so important a person with the ranch. 'You know Joan, back at home the neighbours think he is the owner of the Buckboard'. 'I know that' said Joan, 'they also think he is enticing the youth of Ballygala Parish away and getting the blame for it too. Poor uncle John, he knows about the lack of employment and he would help anyone. But no, he wouldn't tempt them away from their home place'.

'To answer your question Mary, he got his first job here over twenty years ago. He is a hardworking level headed man. Met the bosses daughter at one of the ho-down dances, they fell in love, he married her and got his foot in the door and no better man deserved the chance to go up the ladder. He owns a share in the ranch. But so do a lot of workers own a share, that's why it's such a success, I'm told. That was the way the old man started out over eighty years ago, it's the trend ever since. Workers hired on, buy a share, work on it, but also everyone chips in and work together with the land, the cattle herds, the horses, everything'. 'What a great arrangement,' observed Nora, 'and successful too'.

The Ho-Down

Dancing fever was beginning to hit Nora. 'Oh! For a ceilí, what would I not give for a crack at the floorboards'. 'No Ceilí's here', answered Joan, 'but there is the monthly ho-down'. Nora a step ahead as usual, 'what could we wear to one of them kind of dances'? 'Well', says Joan 'I have been working on that very thing, I asked Livia about the skirts and blouses seeing as we have no money yet we couldn't afford to buy them. No need to worry Joan, come with me to the kitchen she said. She unlocked a big press door. There was dozens of skirts, blouses, waistcoats, petticoats, cowgirl boots and the hats all hung in sections of the various sizes. My I said, does someone have a job to keep them in order? There is about six in staff and the same for the men also says Livia. So I picked out three outfits for us, I have them in the pantry for the next ho-down. It's this Saturday night and by the way Stephen O'Hara wants to know if you will go with him Mary. I think he likes red heads'. 'Oh! No I couldn't' I told her, 'why not yourself Joan?' 'I'm going with my brother Sean and Nora is going with my brother Patsy, his girlfriend Valerie has to work late. So it's our night to have a fling'. 'Since you put it that way tell Mr O'Hara my answer is yes'. Wondering if all new hired hands were taken to ho-downs like that, Joan told me of course not, 'don't forget I'm one of their kinsfolk'. 'I know what you mean' says Nora, 'your uncle owns Buckboard' she laughed. Well I thought it will be something different to walk into a dance hall with a partner. In the old school hall back home you went in with a couple of girls or on your own and looked across to the other side and watch the lads sizing up the girls as they came in the door. Rain or shine we travelled the rough road on our bikes and had good nights dancing the set and then cycle back home again.

Dressing in the ho-down duds as Nora named them was fun. We were transformed in an hour from three Irish Colleens to three Hill Billies. Joan took special care to find me an outfit of green to complement my red hair. 'We must impress Mr O'Hara, he has been here working on the ranch a few years, I bet he would make a good catch'. 'Joan don't make me any more nervous than I already am' I replied. We left the room and headed for our dates as we called them, although I was the only one with a real date. Seeing him striding towards me my heart almost stopped. 'Mary' he said, 'Yes' I said 'and you're Stephen'. 'Aye, that's me'. It was the first time I had met a man that didn't have that Texan drawl.

Getting A Man

What a night that was, we laughed as we fell on the beds. 'I could go to a ho-down every month' says Nora pulling off the cowboy boots. 'The steps are a little bit different to the Ceíli' 'All that clattering of heels, plenty of swinging', put in Joan. 'We had better shower and get to bed'. 'Early morning work' I reminded them. 'Did you get a man Nora'?, asked Joan. 'Thanks to your brother Pete introducing me to a Pete McInerney from Roscommon, I have a date for next months ho-down. He is a nice sort of guy, not very good looking'. "Now my story' says Joan, 'as we walked in the door, Sean my considerate brother left me standing there, while he went away talking to his friends, I was on my own feeling very awkward until a very Texan guy walked over telling me his name'. 'I'm Jake Toby, would you like to dance this one'? 'I would please, but I've never danced square dancing', 'don't worry' said Jake, 'leave it to me', and I did, we danced the night together, he twirled me up and down the floor. Oh! Girls, what a night, and best of all he is taking me to the next one, a month is a long time". 'Give us your news of the handsome Stephen O'Hara Mary'. 'You'll both think I'm foolish after one night, but gals I'm head over heels in love with this man. He is going to take me for a drive out the country in his jeep my next free day'. 'My but you are a fast worker Mary O'Brien' they chorused.

'The skirts are a perfect fit Joan, do you think we could hold on to them for the next ho-down, save a lot of time fitting and matching them up, I have taken a fancy to my one' says Nora. 'I'm sure it will be fine' says Joan, 'but I'll find out anyway'.

A Spectacular Beauty

A spectacular beauty rising early one lovely sunny morning I decided to leave early for work. As I left my residence which was situated in between the honeysuckle cottages, that were built years before to house the Buckboard employees. Some of the employees are now retired and living out their last days in them. Taking my usual pathway along by the creek about a quarter of a miles walk to the laundry room, which had been well extended from a room that once held two washing machines and a clothes wringer to the vast building it is now as it holds masses of machines for the volume of laundry being turned out today, yet the name laundry room was never changed.

I stood a while; gazing about me, it was the first time I really took full notice of this huge terrain that surrounded the Buckboard ranch, with its beautiful valleys, far off hills, miles and miles of wild shrub and cactus. What a spectacular beauty. In between, land tilled and set out in masses of vegetables, fruit trees and acres of grazing land, the foresight of a young man and his wife who emigrated to these parts to seek his fortune. Buying a piece of ground, cultivating it and continuing on as others joined him, putting their labours together until they built, from a small plot to the vast acreage, this land is now. It has given many people of many cultures a haven to grow and expand a rich living experience, expanding the land to breed cattle, horses, plant and reap their produce, and yielding what is necessary to life.

Trying to visualise the man with the strange name of Vest, I would dearly love to know more about him, even get a glimpse of him. As far as I knew he was very old now and only went out walking in the very early hours of the morning. Still living in a large ranch house with some of his family, the house he built from the small one room hovel he and his wife first lived in.

Amazing I told myself as I gazed around me how one side of the world can become so rich and prosperous while the other side continues to live from hand to mouth.

Looking over a high railing I could see ranch hands exercising some greyhounds, I guessed Buckboard had its own dog track too. Maybe Stephen would take me some night. Everything takes place here, in time I will see more of this enchanting scenery created by God and man, but right now I have a laundry job to do. I must hurry or I'll find myself on the boat back to dear old Ireland.

Letter Writing

It gave me a feeling of closeness to mam and home with writing news of the Buckboard and the dance, telling mam about Stephen O'Hara and how he is Irish, I know she will be happy with that information. The year is almost up and soon we will be collecting our pay mam, the dollars, the thought of having money in my hand gives me a thrill. The year went fast after all. Telling mam the Considines were only shareholders in the Ranch and not the owners. Mam would answer my letter by return post. Her latest news was that Sean Considine would be coming home within the year. His Dad will be glad of that; for he didn't like him to emigrate.

After three years on the ranch he won't be coming empty handed. I hear he didn't have to work the year without pay like you did Mary, his Uncle John would have seen to that. Don't breathe a word of that to anyone. Imagine the Considines are only shareholders, everyone here thinking they were big ranch owners in Texas. John did well marrying into something big like that, he was always a hard worker, them Considines are shrewd people. Of course Brid wouldn't like to hear me saying that. She still blames Joan for enticing you away. Mam was indeed great with the home news. Her sad news was that John Kelly's father died without making the peace with his son. I hope Brid and yourself will be sensible and make your peace soon, she didn't go to either the wake or funeral. Of course she wouldn't want to run into John it would open up old wounds. I'm glad you have a nice young man she wrote, is he Catholic Mary? I knew she would ask that question. In my next letter I'll tell her he is Catholic, put her mind at ease.

Pay Day

Queuing for our first pay packet was exciting, chatting and planning how we were going to share it out, 'I'll send some home to mam, buy some nice colours of wool, send to my sister Brid. I'm going to open a savings account in the Buckboard bank have a little nest egg. What's left I'll treat myself to something Texan'. 'It's a good thing we get fed here' says Joan 'or you would be going hungry for the next month'. Nora moaned, 'will there be a pay envelope for us when we reach that window? Look at the line of people ahead of us. I see our two friends Livia and Janice almost at the pay out window'.

'Of course there will be a packet for us, didn't we get notified to be here' answered Joan. 'Remember queuing for our brown envelope at the woollen mill' says Nora with a dreamy look in her eyes. 'Wouldn't this remind you of it'? 'Look Nora snap out of it, we're a long way from the woollen mill', we reprimanded her. 'Alright' she snapped back, 'don't you two ever dream'?

Running with our pay packets straight to our room we were in good humour. Opening it we shouted 'a hundred dollars'. Joan took out some cold drinks from the ice box, getting three glasses she poured the orange drink into them, 'lets celebrate', a slice of chocolate cake did the trick. Inviting the two Italian girls to join us. 'We know how you feel' said Jessica. 'We were excited with our first pay too'. 'Joan's first spending was going on a pair of cowgirl boots'. Asking Nora about her plan, 'see this head of black curls, it's over a year since I had it cut, so girls I'll be unrecognisable next time you all see me'. 'What is your plan Mary'? 'Well I am sending ten dollars to mam, that will get her seven shillings an six pence. Then some wool for Brid, and open an account for me'. 'My goodness', says Joan, 'our Mary is gone all sensible on us'.

Wedding Plans

Surprise shot across everyone's face as I made my announcement. 'Next year prepare yourselves for a wedding'. Running across the room to hug me the girls thought this was wonderful news. 'Mrs Stephen O'Hara' they chorused. 'Easy girls, you'll smother me' I choked. 'Mary, you're going to be the first of us to say I do. Breaking up our threesome'. 'Ah! Girls you won't be long behind me'. 'Where do you think you'll live Mary'? 'Stephen has an eye on one of them new houses they're building down by Spring Hope'. 'He must have money Mary'? 'He is here over five years, how did he get away without meeting someone before now'? Nora wanted to know. 'I asked him that question too, smiling he said, I was waiting for a pretty red head'.

'Well Mary, all joking aside we wish you good luck. Is Spring Hope very far from here Mary'? 'Do you know the old house down by Scrag Hill where they accommodate the retired workers that have worked all their lives on the ranch, well just beyond them about two miles if you ever take a walk down there you'll see some of the old folk sitting outside their doors sunning themselves. The little houses on Honeysuckle Row, there's a few living out their old age there too'. 'Them little cabins are very old', observed Nora. 'How good of the old man Vest to think of an idea like that'.

'I don't think my Pete would ever like to settle here' announced Nora, 'he has a great longing for the ould sod'. 'Why is that'? I asked 'sure we all long for home, but it's here the money is. He could work his fingers to the bone back home and still have nothing'. 'Girls, Pete's only interest is to have enough money to build a good house in his native Roscommon'. 'He sounds like a rock of sense, hold on to him Nora. If, and I say if he does go back will you go back with him'? 'I can't imagine my life without him' smiled Nora. Next we turned to Joan who was sitting very quiet, 'any plans going on with yourself and Jake? I guess he will buy his own ranch being a Texan'. 'Not a chance, he hates ranch work, his secret ambition is to move to Hueston about a couple of hundred miles from here'. 'Joan you wouldn't do that'? I said. 'Well we're not sure yet, he intends to design cowboy memorabilia, buckles, bits spurs, half chaps, all that kind of thing'. 'Wow', echoed Nora, and I together, 'it looks like I'm going to be the only ranch hand left here' I moaned. 'We don't know yet, Jake could still change his mind, at the moment its only talk'. Tears sting my eyes as I look back on the days we sat talking and planning our future with the young men in our lives. Never realising that life and times would set us three lovely lassies so far apart. So much we accomplished in them years and yet we came to this land of plenty from a poor and impoverished beginning.

Mary's Wedding Day

'**T**ime has a way of its own for dealing with things and years creep up on one', my mothers saying, how true that is. Remembering how quickly my own wedding day came round, it dawned bright and early, the sun streaming in across the room, the rays bringing to life the pale green of my wedding dress with the dark green shamrocks trimming the hem.

The two bridesmaids dresses, in a delicate shade of primrose with the deep yellow shamrock trimming there hems. Three sprays of white daisies lay across the mirror waiting to adorn our hair. Looking around me I wondered where Joan and Nora had gone. The door opened and they both came in carrying a silver tray laden with fruit, boiled eggs, toast, a silver teapot of tea, china cups, saucer, sugar and creamer. 'Look' says Nora, 'the bride to be, still lying in bed the most exciting day of her life'. Sampling the fruit and sipping the tea gingerly from such a pretty china cup I felt like a queen. 'Here' says Joan 'I'll top your egg, so eat up and we'll dress you in your wedding outfit'.

'My thanks to you both but you shouldn't, you're both so good to me' I said through sniffles. 'We know you're thinking of your mother. Sure she couldn't come all that journey'. 'Did I show you the wedding gift she sent to me'. 'No you didn't' they echoed. 'Look a white Irish linen table cloth and six napkins'. 'It's beautiful Mary' the girls said looking down at the linen cloth, 'here's a little card, it says "my blessings to you both and thank you Mary for all the dollars, love you mam"'.

'Your mam has good taste'. 'She always had Joan' I said. 'I remember Christmas time how she would buy the lovely flowery oil cloth for the kitchen table and the matching strip for across the mantel piece with the bevelled edge. I would sit for hours counting all the flowers and their colours. Remember the big red Christmas candle, it was my job to light it on Christmas Eve and place it on the window sill.

I miss the lovely juicy goose mam would stuff with potato stuffing it was rich and daddy would bring in an arm full of turf and pile the sods against the hearth wall'. Joan and Nora sat quietly as I sobbed for my past life and home. Then good old Nora came on with a verse from a poem we learned in school:

'Oh! To have a little house
To own the hearth and stool and all
The heaped up sods upon the fire
The pile of turf against the wall'

'Now' says Joan 'that's enough of that I hope, you have all your crying done now Mary, it wouldn't do to be walking down the aisle with tears streaming down your lovely cheeks, remember these lines. Thy fate is the common fate of all into each life a little rain must fall' - how true.

Now as I recall them times I get up from the chair opening the press drawer I take out the Irish linen table cloth, hold it to my cheek and think on the years I put it on the table as Stephen and myself celebrated our wedding anniversaries, twenty five of them, now mam both you and Stephen are gone to your great reward.

As for me all I have is reflecting back to bygone times. Our wedding was a big event in this far away land. Saint Matthew's Church was full. Walking down the aisle on the arm of Joan's uncle John Considine; who proudly handed me over to my husband to be in his dark green suit and white dickie bow. Joan's brothers Sean and Pete acting as bestman and usher wore cream suits and green ties, how handsome they both looked. My two bridesmaids, Joan and Nora coming behind me, were looking stunning. Father Jerome giving us his blessing complemented the beautiful Irish wedding. And the bride with her bridesmaids, dressed in their contrasting symbols of shamrocks in green and gold colours. I look and see that wedding photo hanging on my kitchen wall. And think of the notable contrast of a marriage in Texas and at home in the old country when I was growing up, the two people getting married, the witnesses and the priest to perform and bless the marriage. The meaning was the same but far from being so elaborate. The couple went home to a good breakfast, which some kind neighbours would have cooked for them. The couple changed out of their wedding attire, his suit, her costume (jacket, skirt and blouse) these clothes did them for years after. No honeymoon for them, it was working as usual. Stephen and I had going away outfits to honeymoon in Florida for two weeks.

Remaining on as head laundress, I continued to work. Stephen and I were living in one of the Honeysuckle Cottages until our house was built. My days sharing the room with Joan and Nora were now over; as I thought about that it was another turning point in our lives, a constant changing that we would get used too. I was happily married to Stephen, but I couldn't resist contemplating on the times the three of us spent together. Stephen bought his own ranch, an extension of the great Buckboard, now we need a name for it, I thought.

Another Wedding

One morning working in the laundry I thought I heard my name called over the noise of the washing machines. 'It's yourself Joan'. 'It is'. 'I knew I would find you here, you have news then', 'I have' she said, 'I'm here looking for a maid of honour for my wedding and you, Mrs O'Hara are the perfect person'. 'There's a wedding brewing' I said in surprise. 'Yes there is, Jake and I are getting married in two months time, I want to be a June bride'.

'But Joan, you have two cousins, your uncle John's daughters, would you not like to have one of them a Chief Bridesmaid'. 'No it's you I want. Nora and my two cousins will be bridesmaids. I have most of the bridal outfits got, come over to the room and I'll show them to you, you're wearing deep blue; it will set off your red hair. Bridesmaids are in pale blue'. 'And your own gown Joan?' 'I hope you like it Mary, it's a cream colour with a row of pearl beads around the hem. We will have a fitting this evening, be sure to come'. 'I will indeed, Mrs Jake Tolby'. 'I'll be leaving from Uncle John's house, unlike you, you left from this room on your wedding morning'. 'I did, but then Joan you are kin folk. When did you decide to get married so soon'? 'A couple of months ago. My brother Sean is going home real soon and I want him to give me away. Dad is in failing health, poor man'. 'Another Irish wedding' says Father Jermome 'and within a few months of each other too. I'm very honoured to be marrying John Considine's niece, Joan to this handsome Texan. I've known John for many years, a very respectable parishioner. So this day does me proud'.

Joan's wedding was spectacular, her uncle and his wife Maisie put everything into it. Although we never heard or seen much of Maisie who was the true blood connection of the Buckboard ranch, still she seen to Joan's wedding.

The flowers were deep and pale blue with cream roses. Joan in her cream dress, Jake in a cowboy suit including fringed waist coat and high heel cowboy boots, the bestman was Joan's brother Sean and Jake's three brothers dressed in contrast with the groom; they were very handsome in their glittering attire. After the reception we ate and drank and danced the square dances. Afterwards, Joan and Jake left for Niagara Falls on their honeymoon. 'Goodbye Mr & Mrs Jake Tolby' we were all shouting and throwing packets of rice after them.

Nora and Mary have a Chin Wag

Heading to work one sunny morning, going along by the creek. Our temporary residence was a nice little stroll. Our own house was not yet complete. Stephen had some finishing touches to put to it in his own liking. Hearing a shout across the lawn it was Nora, out for a break deciding to stroll around the lawn. 'Good morning Nora' I said, 'shouldn't you be in at work in the nursery'? 'The supervisor suggested I take some fresh air, she's breaking in new staff'. 'Does that mean you are going to get a promotion Nora'? 'I'm hoping for that. I could do with a change'. 'What time do you start in the mornings Nora'? 'Six o'clock, a promotion would mean an eight o'clock start'. 'The same as me now as I'm the head laundress, it's an eight o'clock start, some evenings it can be very late though when I finish after showing new people the works program'.

'Tell me Nora, has anyone taken my place in our room to keep you company'? 'Well Mary with the two Italian girls speaking their own language when they're together, I will soon have two German women, one already moved in and using what used to be your side of the room, her friend will join us in a couple of weeks and take over Joan's part of the room. Then I guess they will talk in their own language. I will be talking to myself. The lady who has moved in, her name is Elsa, loves to chat which is good, she has been a waitress for forty years in the big house. Her friend is also a waitress, they will soon be retiring'.

Elsa's Past

'Telling me she never married was as good as your sister Brid's let down. I wish you could have heard her tell how she got let down years ago in Germany'. 'What happened in her love life'? I was keen to know. 'She was engaged to Fran, a handsome blonde, blue eyed German. She couldn't describe this handsome beauty enough. They were a year engaged. Making plans to set up home, money was scarce, but Elsa was putting aside every mark she earned for their big day'. There were tears in her eyes telling me what happened. 'Come on Nora, what happened to the engagement'? I quizzed. 'Well one evening he came to her house dressed in army uniform. She got a shock. Fran, she said, you never said you were enlisting in the army, explaining to me the shock she got. Why don't you wait until we are married, and I can travel with you as your wife? No Elsa; it's better this way he told her. Army wages are good, we will save more, much quicker for our wedding day. When he put it like that I agreed half heartedly. How long will you be away? Two years, I'll write you all the time and come home on leave; the two years will just fly. Is it dangerous, where you are going to be stationed? Not really my love, he answered. Saying our sad goodbyes was breaking my heart, seeing tears in his eyes gave me much grief. I worked hard as a waitress so I didn't mind being in every night, I was company for my parents. Fran wrote to me every week pouring out his love and I replied in the same way. Then Nora, she said his letters became fewer and fewer. I put it down to the war. I guessed he was being shifted to different troubled areas. One morning my mother said, Elsa, there's a young army man in the living room, he wants to talk to you. Going into the room, I feared my Fran was killed in action, then I thought he was injured. I will look after him for the rest of my life. Thinking of him being brought off the plane in a stretcher, my handsome soldier. The army man stood as I entered the room. He looked unofficial to me. I thought Fran was neither injured nor dead. Introducing himself saying, you may guess this is not an official call. I'm in

Fran's squadron, he asked me to bring a message to you Miss Elsa. Please sit down, he said you are engaged to each other. Yes we are to marry in about two years. You may need your mother with you to hear this news. Calling mother in I said this soldier has a message for me from my fiancé; he wants you here with me to hear it. Sitting on the arm of my chair she put her arm around me, she realised the news before I did. The last words I heard were Fran married an army cadet a month ago, he is very much in love with her and he is sorry. The next thing I was aware of was my dad sprinkling water on my face. Mother patting my hands, the messenger was gone. I was days in bed, I was like a zombie Nora. Phone calls were coming from the café for me to appear for work. Go to your work Elsa says dad, tomorrow you get out of that bed and pull yourself together and go to your work. He spoke in such an authoritative tone, I did exactly as he said, I'm glad I listened to him. The rest is history. Nora, I wish Brid could meet Elsa, they have something in common. Disappointments like that can happen anywhere in the world. At the time, the person thinks they're the only one with a big heart break'. The conversation changed.

'They're going to knock the Honeysuckle Cottages where Stephen and I are living temporarily. They're replacing them with up to date apartments'. 'I know Mary, Elsa says herself and her friend will be getting one of them when they're fully retired, her friends name is Olga. They will be both sharing what we used to call our room. I'll be listening to two Italians and two Germans conversing in their own language, I'll be talking to myself. Oh! I do miss you and Joan'. Hugging Nora I said 'it won't be long until yourself and Pete ties the knot too. Where are the Italian girls, I haven't seen them since my wedding'? 'They finish work so late in the kitchen; they shower, change their clothes and then go meet their dates. How clever of you Livia I said, it's the only way she said, we spend our days off in bed, we're that tired. We copped on to the idea when we seen other kitchen staff doing it. Its big news with Livia herself and her boyfriend are planning to go to New York and open a pizzeria parlour there, they would do well there. 'Will Jessica go with them' I asked? 'She's not too fond of kitchen work; she says my hands, my hands, they sore all the time, they sore, I need change of job'. 'We had better get to our own jobs Nora. You and Pete call to see me and Stephen some evening'. 'We will Mrs O'Hara' she shouted after me. 'You Devil', I shouted back.

Thinking as I hurried to the laundry. I wonder where herself and Pete will get married? It won't be in Texas I'm quite sure, thinking about Pete, you would know he never really fitted in and it was good he met someone like Nora; she was deep in love with him. If they do go back to Roscommon to marry I won't be there, I got one of my familiar pangs of loneliness. I won't ponder on this I thought to myself, better get on with the laundry, maybe a washing machine or dryer will be broken down; as often happens.

An Emotional Feeling

Putting the final touches to our house Stephen left early, 'the sooner it's finished the sooner we can move in' he said as he kissed me going out the door. No sooner had he left than a strange sad feeling came over me. There's something wrong somewhere I thought. Saying a prayer for it to pass, I continued getting ready for work.

Stepping out the door an eerie feeling gripped me, the yard hands were going about their work quietly. There was no whistling; truck radios normally blaring out cowboy songs were silent. Even the birds didn't seem in the mood for their morning chatter. The few yard hands I did see had black bands around their arms. Looking around I noticed all flags lowered to half mast. From the stars and stripes to the loan star Texas flag and all the flags representing the different nationalities employed in the past and present at the Buckboard ranch. Walking down by the creek to the laundry room, black bands were wrapped around hitching posts; railings; gates; black crepes were pinned to every door on the ranch. It could mean only one thing, the Lord of the Manor known as 'Vest' had passed away. Moving closer to the Ranch house I could see a group of yard hands polishing the most splendid harness ever seen. Such was the décor that adorned it, four horses heads of pure gold stood at each corner on the hearse roof. Across the hearse was a framework depicting a ranch with miniature farm features assembled to honour the great man and what he stood for.

Six handsome black horses were being groomed until their coats shone like glass. Black harnesses trimmed with gold were being placed on their backs, black plumage attached to their elegant heads and horseshoes studded with sparkling studs. Gazing on all this eloquence and thinking what pomp and splendour, suddenly a great bell boomed out a forlorn sound across the Buckboard Ranch. As it boomed out its last chord a loudspeaker took over, 'calling all Buckboard employees to assemble in the El Paso Hall within the hour. Everyone please be present to receive instructions to prepare a farewell to a great man who passed away in his sleep early this morning'.

Instead of going to the laundry I went to the El Paso Hall, already a great gathering of workers were assembled there. Men were wearing black bands around their hats or on their sleeves. Searching for Stephen, I wondered where he was. I could not see him among the crowd. Many stood with heads bowed, some drying their eyes, it was indeed a sad day. The principle organiser stepped forward calling for a minute's silence. Then he called each charge hand to come forward instructing each one to select his helpers to take charge of the various assignments necessary for the funeral. Calling a man named Hank, the head of coaches. As Hank called his men to assemble at the stables I was proud to hear my husbands name been called. Knowing that Stephen would be driving a horse drawn coach I would be walking on my own behind the hearse, once again in a different country in a totally different situation in comparison to my dear Fathers funeral, his was a horse drawn cart, and his coffin placed across it. There was no pomp for him, I'm sure he went to heaven too, in his own way he was a kind and good man, whom we loved and missed dearly.

Lying in State

The fabulous trimmed lawn lay like a carpet in front of the great mansion. Here is where the old gentleman's remains lay in state, while family members; employees of every creed and description; and mourners from miles away filed past the magnificent casket placed on a jet black Bier. A large wooden box stood beside the casket for the Mass cards, and floral wreaths adorned the lawn. Seats for those who wished to sit and keep the deceased company for hours, whilst ranch hands passed cold drinks around. The final prayers were offered by Father Jerome.

Last Journey

Then as the hearse and six black horses and two foot men in black, wearing tall hats led the large cortege of coaches, carrying family members which indeed were many. Ranch hands walked either side in a guard of honour. Thousands walked the distance to Saint Matthews Church where Bishop Joseph Russell stood waiting in his magnificent robes flanked by several priests befitting this occasion to welcome the remains of the great man who, through his years, built up the Buckboard ranch to what it has become this very day. Making our way gently, behind the slow movement of the horse drawn hearse, I was lucky to see Nora in the crowd. I hurried my steps to be with her. While we walked side by side we talked of the grandeur of the funeral so far, gazing at the awe-inspiring trail of horse drawn coaches in their splendour. 'It's going to be a long ceremonial service' moaned Nora. 'Oh! Nora' I said, 'don't you think the good man is worthy of a long ceremonial send off'?

A final stop before we entered the church which was big enough to be called a Cathedral, a lady in black came hurrying towards us wearing a black hat with a veil covering her face. As she came nearer we realised it was Joan. 'You're all in black Joan'! 'Yes, you see Uncle John's wife gave strict orders all kin folk must dress in black'. 'Your dress is lovely' said Nora, 'but a bit too tight'. 'There's good reason for that'. 'Don't tell me Joan' I said, 'you're expecting, and I'm six months married before you and not a sign yet'. 'Don't worry Mary, it will happen' she assured me. 'As for me I would have preferred if Jake and myself were settled in our new home before I got pregnant, but we are both very happy about the baby coming. I'm very glad I'm here for the old mans funeral, and maybe you will still be here at the Buckboard for the birth and we can look forward to the christening. I hope I am, but Jake is itching to get his business up and going. Having seen the harness and hearse trimmings he is already advancing his ideas still further for his equine designs'.

Slowly entering this huge church of Saint Matthews, we wondered would there be room for the massive crowd who followed the pole bearers as they carried the pure oak casket slowly down the aisle and then placing it on the bier before the altar. While organ music rang out and flowers bedecked the altars; many candles could be seen lighting throughout the church, inhaling their heavy waxen scent. Nora couldn't let an opportunity pass as she remarked our Christmas candle never smelled that strong. 'Nora dear' I said with a smile, 'you just said that with a Texan drawl'. 'I'm catching it' she whispered, at this we smothered a laugh.

Margaret Dowling

Funeral Mass

Saint Matthew's Church fell silent as his Lordship Bishop Joseph Russell mounted the altar. Welcoming everyone who came to pay their last respects to a great man. A very young man named Silvester Harris, affectionately known as 'Vest' (I turned to Nora and whispered 'that's where the 'Vest' comes in'). The Bishop continued to give the history of the late Silvester's life. It's many years ago since as a young man with his young wife Abigail left Australia to seek their fortune in a new land, like many of you good people who are here today. How fortunate we were that they chose this part of Texas. Working hard to eke out a living in what was then a barren and wild ground with every dollar he made he bought another piece of ground and hired another hand to help turn it into what it is today and naming it the Buckboard Ranch. Hard work and rearing eight children, four sons and four daughters was a hard and busy life for the Harris's. The oldest son Matthew is seated before me in the front pew in his eightieth year. His Father Silvester Harris now departed from this life in his hundred and fifth year was a man before his time. With a foresight for, and a love of land. As busy people they were not without their love for fun and enjoyment. With the help of the ranch hands they built an entertainment facility which Abigail named El Paso Hall. There many a sweetheart met their future spouse. As we observe the many national flags from the stars and stripes to the Texas lone star flying at half mast for the past week in solemn honour. He expressed his love of mankind by honouring them in flying the flag of their country, it can be well seen the many different nationalities he employed at the Buckboard Ranchland, also encouraging the many cultures to be expressed, in this way people brought a piece of themselves to remind them of their homeland enriching and nurturing the great expanse of cultivated ground we see before us today. Many a man and woman he has given a start in life. Proudly I stand here knowing I too served my time in the Buckboard Ranch. Driving steers from acre to acre, mucking out horse stables to help pay for my college education, yes that is correct, many a priest before you on this altar today can boast the same privilege. He never forgot the hardworking hands that served him, by building the Honeysuckle Cottages to accommodate the old retired hands who were unable to provide for themselves in those bygone days. He was a believer in doing the humane thing. The cottages are still in use for those waiting to move to their own home. Times have changed for the better, the old and infirm are not as neglected, thank God for that. I could go on for hours singing his praises, many accolades you will hear as Mass progresses in his honour. The great man's slogan ('you're not a man unless you share with your fellow man and always keep your promise'). This he put into practice and passed it onto his family. The great man is today with his Abigail and his Creator.

Reap and multiply as Silvester and Abigail did. Abigail bore eight children, four sons and four daughters. Their children between them increased the family by sixty grandchildren. They in turn have increased the family with eight great grandchildren and the latest five great great grandchildren. Would you like me to go on? The Church erupted in loud applause. Silvester outlived his Abigail by twenty years, she died aged eighty five. Like many of the hired hands who cultivated this land for some this was the only home they knew, therefore he established Buckboard Graveyard where he will be laid to rest beside his Abigail, and in the company of those poor souls. Turning to Nora I whispered 'my Dad must be still standing outside the pearly gates'. 'Why'? she asked? 'He only managed to produce two of us and never a grand child yet'. 'Oh! Would you stop? But all in all wasn't Vests life history brilliant'? I agreed. The solemn requiem mass got underway by chief celebrant Bishop Russell (as Nora said whom we have a lot in common, mucking out horse manure, we had a secret smile at that one). So many priests, I lost count, old, very old and some quite young.

The Church was filled with the heavenly sound of organ music. The beautiful combination of the various choirs. The volume of male tenor almost bringing the roof down and the sweet gentle tones of the female voices, right down to the angelic children's voices. As I looked up at the high altar, I could almost see angels soaring above it, such was the feeling this mass was giving me. Mass now coming to a close, we would soon be heading to the Buckboard graveyard where poor 'Vest' would be laid beside his wife. Nora asking 'did you feel the Mass long'? 'Not really' I answered, 'how long was it'? 'Four hours'! 'Did you think it long Nora'? 'No' she said 'the singing and music was so entertaining and enrapturing'. 'After the burial when the crowd disperses come to my place for a coffee and something to eat Nora'. 'I will, the burial will be another four hours or more'. 'Yes, and a majority will go to the dining hall for food. They're having caterers bring in a steer to feed the masses of people. I have never seen them to use caterers before. The entire employees were at the funeral the full week. The work will all start very early in the morning. I have to go to the laundry tonight to finish any outstanding work load, get started first thing in the morning. All them table cloths, napkins from the official dining room. The altar cloths have to be freshened up. I'll need the staff to clean the candle grease off them. Iron it off with the brown paper over it, I learned that from my mother'.

'Well I had no nursery; the parents were all off and kept the children with them'. Our conversations flowed on as we walked slowly to the final resting place. Again Nora with her wit, 'Mary you had no plumage on your horses head for your fathers, may he rest in peace, funeral'. 'For goodness sake Nora, will you hould your whisht, where would you get plumage in Ballygala'? 'You could have pulled a few feathers from the ganders' tail' Nora said while laughing. 'Oh! Nora my pet, may your sense of humour for ever be with you'.

Reminiscing

My poor mind keeps slipping into the past, then back to the present again. If Stephen was here we would be reminiscing all of our experiences at the ranch too. I remember telling him how proud I was of him as he drove one of the coaches at the old man's funeral. Needless to say I was a bit chuffed myself he smiled.

Thinking back as a poor mill working girl from a remote part of Ireland attending such a splendid funeral, was miles and miles from home, and being part of such an eloquent ritual in the United States of America. The place where anything is possible (if you're willing to work for it). It worked well for the three of us girls, even though Nora and her Pete returned to Ireland. Joan said she would never forget the old mans funeral Mass. Herself and about a dozen more pregnant women had to be seated outside the Church, the scent of the burning wax candles made them sick and a couple of them fainted. We laughed when she said she never wants to see another candle, not even at her funeral.

Joan has her Baby

Jake was working late, he had been in the hospital all night, and then giving Stephen his big news, Joan gave birth to a baby son. Stephen lost no time in coming to the laundry to tell me the news. I was happy for the Toby's. 'How much did he weigh'? 'I don't know'. 'What are they going to call him'? 'I don't know'. 'God Stephen, did you ask Jake anything, how is Joan? Don't answer that'. 'Mary I rushed here to tell you the good news'. 'Oh Stephen I'm so excited I hardly know what to say'. Joan and Jake's baby was a big nine pounder, for a first baby he was big, with a mop of black curls and the picture of his daddy. They're naming him Jake Óg, can you believe it.

Myself and Nora were so happy. Joan stayed at the Buckboard to have the baby and then the christening in Saint Matthews. 'I did it Mary because I want you for godmother', once again I enquired 'why not have one of her cousins', 'no' she said, 'they're already godparents to cousins. Jake's brother Vernon will be godfather. After the christening we will leave for Huston'.

Jake Óg's Christening

The christening was a double occasion; Father Jerome was in a celebratory mood. After the sadness of the late Silvester Harris, there's joy in a new birth. It was such a joyous celebration. You could just feel everyone's happiness. 'Joan' I said, 'you always did the thing right'.

After the baby's baptism everyone was invited to the El Paso hall for not just the drink to wet the babies head, but Joan and Jake chose that time to say farewell to their friends. Jake saying farewell, thanked all connected to the Buckboard Ranch for giving himself and Joan a start in life and likewise he expressed his luck in meeting such a beautiful Irish girl who has now presented him with a beautiful baby boy. Myself and Nora stood together supporting each other for the tears were flowing. 'Oh! Dear' says Nora, 'not another American wake. Will you look at the amount of gifts above on the stage Mary; they will never fit in the small suit case'. At this I pulled her into the toilet where we could laugh without drawing attention to our silly selves. We were not alone for very long when Joan popped her head in the door. 'Will you look at the two of them laughing and crying at the one time'. 'Nora says it's another American Wake'. 'She's right there, we will always keep in touch' says Joan. 'And now is as good a time as any Nora, let us in on your and Peter's plans'.

'I'm not supposed to tell anyone' admitted Nora, 'Peter is the kind that doesn't like parties. We are almost ready and packed to leave in a month's time. Peter wants to marry in his own parish of Carona, he has big family of relations and his Mam and Dad are still living. We are going to bring my Mam to live with us, she's selling the little cottage and it will give her a little spending money. Peter is giving in his notice and has asked for no big goodbyes, so we're just going to have a few drinks the night before we leave with our close friends'. I was in a new burst of tears at this latest news. 'I always knew you and Peter would go back to Roscommon, but I didn't expect it to happen so soon'. 'Well' says Joan, 'the three of us are going to have a Nora and Pete toast, so come out of here, we'll go to the bar'.

'I won't be leaving for a week so I want the two of you to come to my place tomorrow, and look over on the stage, all them presents and gifts, I don't need all of them. I want to share them out with ye'. 'Oh! No Joan, I have my place furnished already. Give them to Nora'. 'How would I get them over to Ireland? I have already sent over about ten parcels. They will all be in Pete's dads' garage, there's nowhere else to keep them'. 'Well you can send off ten more' says Joan. 'Have you seen where you're going to be Joan'? 'Only in photos, a four bedroom house, sitting and dining rooms, kitchen, study, big yard to the back, lawn to the front and Jake's harness premises at one of the gable ends. We have a lot of decorating to do on it, priority is the nursery'. 'I was thinking Joan why don't yourself, Jake and Jake Óg come to our house on Friday evening for a going away buffet supper'?

Final Get Together

Come on I want to invite Nora and Pete too. Nora was sure the two German women; her roommates would be delighted to come. 'Here Nora, give this note to Livia and Jessica, I'm asking them too and their boyfriends. I would love to meet the Italian boys. I bet they're real handsome with sloe black eyes'? 'Mary, such thoughts and you a married woman'. 'Stephen is safe Joan. I had a busy few days trying to please everyone's palate. I had roast beef, a variety of salads, and a trifle for afters. I believed no-one had one of these before and a big cake that said Slán Abhaile. It was a beautiful get together, everyone chatting at the same time. The Italian gentlemen were ever so polite, just like their girlfriends Livia and Jessica. Food, drinks and sing songs, everyone singing in their own language. Anthony sang a love song, looking into Livia's eyes, their was love in their hearts'.

We talked well into the night. Little Jake Óg was such a sweet baby, sleeping all through, giving Joan and Jake chatting time. I was interested in finding out how Joan's brother Sean got on with the sheep farming so far. 'I believe it is doing very well. Like yourself Mary, mam is the only one I can get news from'. 'Did your mam tell you my sister Alice got married'? 'No Joan, I haven't heard from my mam in a while'. 'She'll be telling you in her next letter I bet'. 'When did Alice get married'? 'A month ago, she was five months pregnant. Father Clancy read her the riot act, and told her to do the honourable thing, marry the guy, give the baby a name; he didn't have to do that to her, it upset her for days. They were going to get married anyway'. 'Who is her man Joan'? 'He's from Sligo, mam says he is a nice lad, just this happened to poor Alice, now they are both gone to live in Dublin. Mam misses Alice. She's a Mrs Brian Murphy now. I'm going to pack some of these gifts. I don't need so much and send them over to her. Give me her address and I'll send something for the baby, Nora will want to know as well. She will and I haven't told her yet with all that's happening. I remember Alice coming to Queens Town to say goodbye to you. She wondered if my sister Brid would knit her a dressing gown. I wonder if she ever did?'

Well there I go again, all of that was so long ago. The Tolby family moved to Huston Texas. Joan delighted in decorating her new home. The last I heard from her Jake was thriving in his own business with the equine ornaments. They also had an increase in the family, a second son, they named him Stephán. I was now in the early stages of my first pregnancy and couldn't wait to write the news to mam. I knew she would tell Brid she was going to be an auntie.

Mam's Letter

'First I must congratulate you and Stephen on your good news. A new baby and to make me a Grandmother, I'm praying for you Mary. Brid and myself got invited to Nora and Pete's wedding. One of Pete's brothers collected us when he came for Nora's mother. I wish you could have seen Nora coming up the aisle in her white satin dress and flowing veil, she was a vision with her lovely black curly hair. She had two bridesmaids in violet. Violet flowers on the altar, her poor mother looked beautiful in a pale grey suit, a violet hat, gloves, bag and grey shoes.

Pete and Nora splashed out the dollars on their wedding. There was never such a wedding seen in that little chapel and the reception meal (we always called the breakfast) words just wouldn't describe it. The cake Mary was five tiers, violet with white icing. Pete and Nora, Mr and Mrs McInerney arrived in a white limousine, you know Mary, one of them big posh cars. The whole family turned out in grandeur. Even myself and your sister Brid did ourselves proud in our attire. I wore a long blue matching coat and dress. As for Brid, picture her in a yellow suit, yellow and navy hat and accessories to match. After all the celebrating Mary we were sad returning home, for Nora's mother was not with us. She's living with Nora and Pete now, which is nice for her, it would be lonely on her own in the little cottage, it's up for sale now. I'm going to miss her. The times and the place are taking on big changes. Mary, if you ever come back home you won't know poor ould Ballygala.'

Mam always had a longing for me to return home. But as things were not good between Brid and me, I had no wish to return.

Mum's letter continues: 'Joan's dad passed away, and the son Sean has a big sheep farm, plenty of wool for the mill. The mill workers are getting fewer all the time, the ones there can't keep up with the work load. It's only a matter of time before Mr O'Flynn will close the whole place down. There will be no work for Sean's wool supply. He will sell up and move away too. I hear he is great with a teacher in Dublin; he goes up regular to visit his sister Alice and family.

Father Clancy's sister, the local nurse, has transferred to the city, not enough work for her here. She's missed, for she was better than any doctor. Any of us get a little something wrong with us now into hospital they'll shift us. I was saying to Brid, I'm sure poor olde Father Clancy will want a transfer as well now because his sister is moved on. His old car is always breaking down. He can't visit the sick or house bound as often as he would like too. Nora will be sending you some of her wedding photos. She sent one to us; Brid got a lovely frame for it. It's hanging next to the Sacred Heart picture now'. Mam's letter went on at length giving details of the village happenings. She never did mention if Brid got the parcel of wool I sent, I guess she forgot.

We have a Son

Easter Monday morning, my labour pains started. Stephen hurried me into hospital, every turn of the car on the road I thought I would give birth. After the midwife examined me she told Stephen, 'your wife is not ready to give birth yet, so you can go home and we will call you as soon as the baby arrives'. It was easy see the new daddy-to-be was relieved to get away. This is one of the happiest days of my life, the day I became Mrs Stephen O'Hara and today as I hold my new son. You have a lovely healthy baby boy Mary and your husband is on his way.

A tear came from the new daddy's eye as he eased down the blanket to look at his little chubby faced son. 'God bless him, he is beautiful. What will we name him'? 'What do you think of Donnald'? 'Donnald O'Hara sounds a good strong name for the lad'. 'Is there anything you need mammy'? 'There is Daddy, pen, paper, a stamp and envelope, I'll write our news straight away to mam. Will it be time enough to send word to your people when I get home Stephen'? 'I've taken care of that, I sent them a wire on my way here' he said with a big smile. 'I'll tell mam first, then Joan and Nora', the picture of our happy family hanging on the kitchen wall could tell a story too. Father Jerome christened baby Donnald, Livia and her boyfriend, Anthony were his godparents.

It was now a month after I had written the good news to mam and still had no answer back from her. I knew she wouldn't be able to accept the christening invitation. I said to Stephen 'post that for me, it's a letter to Father Clancy. I must find out about mam or I'll go mad'. 'Now Mary, calm down dear'. I remember his words so well. 'The letter probably got mislaid'. 'We'll soon see', I said. And gathering up Donnald to me I began to nurse him, my oh my, he was a hungry baby. Looking down on him I said 'Granny O'Brien knows you're here Donnald and next year we are going over for her to meet you and your Aunty Brid must meet you too'.

Father Clancy's Reply

Father Clancy wrote to me immediately.
Father Tim Clancy
Parish Priest
St Ann's Chapel
Ballygala
Co Clare
Ireland

Dear Mary

Congratulations to you and your husband on the birth of your son Donnald on Easter Monday morning.

At the same time I must convey my sympathy to you on the death of your mother who passed away that same week. She was bedridden for a while. I visited her regularly with the Blessed Sacrament. She had a large wake and a fine funeral. She died in her sleep. Brid took great care of her.

She always spoke well of you and the dollars you sent and knitting wool to Brid. The woollen mill is expected to close soon. Sean Considine sold up, moved to Dublin, married a teacher, and he is studying to do Archaeology, his mother is living with them now.

The Bishop is transferring me to another Parish in the city of Limerick. So this is my last letter Mary.

I remain always your servant

Father Tim

Once more as I've done many a time I go to the drawer, take out Father Clancy's, may he rest in peace, letter that is now yellow with age, re-read it for the hundredth time, the same sad feeling hits me as it did over twenty years ago. All my connections with Ballygala are gone. My sister Brid won't write me. What a sorry isolated person she is. I think to myself, no I mustn't think badly of her. Mam would be hurt ('she is your sister Mary', she would say).

Part Two

Donnald comes to Ireland

In search of his Family Tree

Margaret Dowling

Donnald's Surprise

Donnald will soon come hurrying in for his dinner, with a bang of the door and what's for dinner mom? If he knew the thoughts going on in my head he would have me locked away. Well enough of that now, I reprimanded myself, check on your son's dinner. Bacon, cabbage, boiled potatoes, Irish dinner, he likes it.

For the first time since Donnald's dad passed away I take out mam's wedding present, the white linen table cloth with the six serviettes and set the table with it. The door bangs shut; he is home, 'wash your hands' I tell him. 'I'm a big boy now' he calls back. I smile to myself, you will always be my baby. Sitting at the table he seems preoccupied. 'Hello son, everything alright with you'. I'm startled with his news. 'I've finally made up my mind. I'm going to Ireland. Your part of the old sod first mam, then to the north to visit dad's home place. I must see where my roots started out from'. 'I'm struck dumb Donnald, when did you make that decision son'? 'For the last month I've been preparing, getting passport and sorting out work'. 'Is Madeline going with you'? No, not this time, I must get the feel of things over there myself first. She had Grandparents in Mayo; they're all dead now, all O'Reilly's. Mam, what's the occasion with Irish dinner and white tablecloth'? I took a fit of laughing, 'it's so funny I should have made that dinner, this of all evenings, and you talking of going over to the ould sod. Are you sure you want to do that? You will never find Ballygala'. 'I have a map here mom, trace out as much as you can along the line to the nearest town in County Clare. I can follow to that point; someone will surely have some idea of your parish. I always enjoyed as a young lad listening to you and dad describing ye're homeland. Dad, may he rest in peace, seemed to have come from a fairly well off background, in comparison to you'.

'Yes and that wouldn't be too hard. So when are you going and for how long'? 'I'm flying out this weekend for a month'.

An Irish Dinner

'I'll start to pack a few things mom'. 'Do Donnald, but you will need more than a few things and you will need a big case, you're a big fellow and you will need heavy warm clothes. No central heating in County Clare, maybe up the North, your father's people will have all them comfortable conveniences installed'. 'I have my heavy jacket and a few pairs of jeans, some socks and underwear and night shirt, what more do I need? Toiletries, I think I won't bother shaving, who can guess Madeline might fancy me with a beard'. 'Donnald son, don't let this Irish trip turn your head. Where are you planning to go first? North or South'? 'South mom, into Shannon, hire a car, then try to follow the road map'. 'You'll need to watch what side of the road you're driving on too son, I will be worrying about you'. 'No need for worry I will take my time, get the feel of things'.

'Will you visit your Aunty Brid'? 'I sure will, in fact I'm looking forward to meeting her'. 'You're a brave man indeed. Sit into the table and we'll tuck into this gorgeous Irish dinner on the Irish linen tablecloth. Here's a toast, good luck son and may the Irish roads rise to meet you'. 'Oh mom' says Donnald, with a big laugh, 'you can take the man out of the bog but you can't take the bog out of the man, so it is with you mom'. With that we each ate the dinner in silence, each with our own thoughts.

Margaret Dowling

Donnald Arrives in Ireland

As the plane descended slowly over Shannon airport Donnald kept peering out the side window, it was early morning, never did he see such lush green fields, it was the greenest green he ever set eyes on. What a rich green land this is, I'm going to enjoy my stay, he thinks out loud to himself. As the plane touched down the sun was just peeping out from behind the clouds, 'it's going to be a good fine day' he heard a man behind him say. 'That's a good start' he whispered to himself.

Having gone through customs and pulling his big case which his mother packed so carefully for him he headed for the exit to find the hired car. A young man greeted him, 'Donnald from Texas' he shouted. 'Yes, that's me'. 'Ok Sir, here's the keys, sign there, you'll find the car over there' and with that he was gone.

As Donnald approached the little blue Ford he wondered if even one of his legs would fit in it never mind his whole body and the big case. It took a lot of pushing to get the case into the little boot. Now to get myself in, with a lot of effort he finally got his big body in behind the wheel, pushing in the key, turning it, the engine gave a gentle purr. 'Sounds alright' he said to himself, glancing out the side door, he noticed two men staring at him, giving a nod to them he greeted them with a 'top of the morning to you all', 'and the same to yourself Sir' they answered back. With a big wide grin one of them shouted to him, 'did you bring the little car over in your pocket'? Having made their joke they walked away laughing.

I must remember 'Irish humour' he thought to himself. I guess I will have a full month of it. Driving away from the airport and repeating his mothers advice, keep to the left side of the road. Soon he was coasting along, glancing to left and right and taking in as much of the scenery as he could.

A herd of cows was been driven by a farmer ahead of him now, 'how do I slow down'? 'Change gears' it said in the ford manual. Shouting out the car window at the farmer, 'fine herd of steer you have there Sir'. 'What's that you said Sir'? 'I said a fine herd of cattle Sir'. 'No they're cows, I'm a dairy farmer'. 'Good luck Sir'. Oh dear God, I'm only four hours in Ireland and I'm already getting the dialect wrong. Driving on some more, stopping here and there, taking snapshots of old thatch houses, men saving hay in the fields, donkeys drawing small carts, now he was really enjoying himself. Talking with this one and that one. In one small town he saw a pub with the word Guinness over the door. I'll try this Guinness stuff my mother often spoke of. 'A glass of your Guinness' he said to the bar tender. 'Sure Sir, one pint of Guinness coming up'. This he felt was a friendly place, three or four old men sat by a fire smoking pipes and drinking pints. Joining them for conversation, he soon felt these old seasoned guys were quicker with their questions than he was with answers. Getting up to leave he asked the bar tender to pour the four of them a pint each, leaving the money on the counter he waved goodbye to them, for this they won't forget me.

Now at last he was getting a better feel of the road. It was beginning to get dark and he was feeling hungry. Stopping to check the map he felt he was going in the right direction for Ballygala. Slowly coasting along the narrow tree lined road where the trees were like a canopy reaching across from each side as if holding each others branches as if they were hands. The lights of the car could only focus so far out along the winding road. Realising it had become very late and now quite dark, although the clouds were racing across the sky, the moon was beginning to shine through. Now it was very late and he was both hungry and jet lagged, glancing at the petrol gauge and talking to himself, 'why didn't I get gas when I stopped for the pint, listening and answering them old guys questions. I got side tracked, now I'm not sure if I am on the right road to Aunties'.

Donnald loses his Way

The needle is almost down at empty. Where am I? What if the car conks out? I'll freeze to death or die of hunger. Checking my watch, 2am. Mom packed plenty of heavy clothes for me, she knew what she was doing. Slowly driving along in the hopes of seeing some sign of a house, realising it was quite a while since he had seen one. Coming to a t-junction, slowly stopping the car. If I'm having a mirage I'll know I'm in the fairies for I'm sure, that's a light I see at the top of the hill. Driving to the top of the hill, he saw just a small gate, which leads to an open door in a small thatch cottage. The car conked out. Easing his big frame out of the tiny car he pushed the squeaky little gate open. An elderly man came to the door. 'Good night young man, what are you doing in this remote place'? 'I've run out of gas for the car'. 'Gas sir, what is that'? 'I mean petrol! Where can I get some'? 'The old man laughed, you won't get any at this hour of the morning and the nearest place is six or seven miles away'. A female voice came from inside the dimly lit little kitchen.

Finding Hospitality

'**W**ho are you talking to out there Mick'? 'It's a young man who's run out of petrol for his car. I think he is a bit lost'. 'Ask him in will you Mick. Don't be leaving him standing out there. Come in'. 'Thank you' I said. Bending almost in two to get in the door. 'Good night, I'm sorry to bother you at this hour of the morning, but I've lost my way. I'm looking for Ballygala, my mother; Mary O'Brien came from there, her sister Brid still lives there'. 'This is my husband Mick', she said, and asking him, 'do you know the place Mick? I've heard the name before alright, but the name O'Brien escapes me'. 'I should have introduced myself, I'm Donnald O'Hara from Texas, I just arrived in Ireland today, I guess I should say yesterday I'm in search of my family roots'. 'We're pleased to make your acquaintance, I'm Eileen, and this is my husband Mick Ryan. Sit down; would you like a mug of tea'? 'That would be just great'. Fixing the black kettle on a hook over the fire, with the smoke travelling up around its spout making its way up the chimney. I thought what kind of tea would come out of that as it bubbled and boiled over, she lifted it down and made the tea in an even blacker teapot. Watching all this I thought, mam in your many reminiscences of the ould country's way of life, I never took it as fact. Until I see it now in reality. (Oh! For a mug of strong black coffee). The chair I'm sitting on is made of straw; it's so low to the floor my two knees are up to my chin. The good woman poured me a big mug of tea. Smoke or no smoke I'm hungry enough to eat the bloody mug. Sipping at the tea it tasted fine. Eileen then reached to the top of the dresser with all its blue willow patterned plates, probably the richest possession they own. Taking down the blackest baking pan I ever seen, she left it on the table, cutting a good square of apple cake, putting it onto a plate and leaving a fork beside it. Thinking to myself, you might live in the mountain, but you have some learning? 'I hope you like my baking' she says, 'apple cake is his favourite', beckoning her head towards Mick. Looking at the piece of apple cake I wondered what this is going to taste like. Taking a little piece I tasted it. Never had I tasted such heavenly apple cake in my life. Mother makes apple pie, but no way would it compare to this.

As I feasted on the cake and tea she poured me cup after cup. Only the black baking pan was safely on the top of the dresser. I dare not ask for another square, it was Mick's favourite. As I ate I had a good conversation with Eileen. 'Are ye normally up this late'? 'No' she said, 'we go to bed after we say the rosary around ten o'clock'. I thought plenty of bed time loving; only I didn't see any sign of children around the little kitchen. 'It's the cow, she's in calf, and the same cow always has trouble trying to calve. Roars for hours then goes quiet again for maybe a couple of hours. Roaring again for a long time before she finally drops the calf, then she's ok'. 'Do all cows do that over here'? 'No we have three other cows you'd never hear much from them. Only from that poor creature, himself is always worrying about her, of course he doesn't want to loose either one, it just exhausts him, he is not so young at sixty. These parts and hard work ages a man'. 'I understand' I said, thinking to myself, I thought him seventy. 'What does the vet think is wrong with the cow'? 'Well the first year he was concerned he thought he would have to cut her open, and giving her an injection only quietened her down for a bit. Then when it wears off she's worse than ever. So the vet said leave her, we'll let nature take its course. But she has to be watched in case of strangulation; after she has the calf she's as calm as ever poor Bess'. My I thought what affection for their animals.

'I didn't hear her since I arrived', 'She had just calmed down, and she could go all night now without a sound. That would give himself a chance to sleep. We will get you petrol in the morning; I think there is a can handy somewhere'. 'I'll get it myself if you tell me where to go'. 'Don't worry about it, Mick will hop on the bike, go down to Flannery's, he would enjoy a few words with olde Gilbert at the garage'. Just then Mick came in, 'she's quiet now again for a while, I think I'll go and get some shut eye. But first I'll put some more turf on the fire, build up a bit of heat. I'll put a couple of chairs in front of it, you can settle there for the night Donnald'.

I was just about to say 'thank you Mick that will do me fine'. When Eileen says, 'well you will do no such a thing Mick, a big man like him sitting all night on two chairs'.

'It's alright I tried to say'. 'Where will he go? asks Mick. 'He can sleep in our bed, it's plenty big enough'. 'What'? says Mick. 'He can sleep next to the wall and you can go in the middle of the bed'. 'But Eileen, where are you going to sleep'? 'Mick, I always sleep out on the edge of the bed and that's where I'll sleep tonight too. So go on, take the young man out and show him where he can do his business, then off to bed with the two of ye, I'll light a candle and leave it in the room for ye with the moon light that's shining into the room tonight ye won't need a candle for long'.

Following Mick out the door and bending as low as I could to fit through without banging my head ('Jaysus mom, where did you come from'? I said to myself.)

Mick led me to the gable end of the house 'over here to the ditch and you can let splash. If you want to do the other, you can go into the cowshed; Eileen always has some newspapers left down there. We have no lavatories in these parts'. 'Thanks Mick, that will do'. 'Jaysus mother', you warned me, but not enough.

Now for the bed (three in a bed and the little one said.....). The last time I slept three in a bed was between mam and dad and she'd sing that rhyme to me. I used to love the rolling over part and the two of them would squeeze me between them, how old was I, three or four years old??

'Good night to ye. I'll tidy up here and I'll get a little rest too. The cow will surely start as soon as my head hits the bolster'. 'Good night Eileen'. Remembering his mom once telling him the first time she slept on a mattress was on the boat going to America. In her home it was a feather tick it was cosy but sometimes the feathers would gather in one place and her mam would shake it up to make it comfortable again.

Eileen's Thoughts

The kitchen now to herself, Eileen sat down, her thoughts on the gorgeous handsome Prince lying in her bed. Oh! How she would love one cuddle with him, picturing his strong arms around her, his legs, oh! Those long legs.

I'd better clear my mind of such thoughts. The cow will start to roar any minute now, the only creature to roar in labour around here. Mick, she couldn't find fault with him, he saved her in her young life from a demon of a father, and she could never forget that for him. Marrying a man twenty years older than herself didn't bother her back then. Their first few weeks of married life was exciting, she enjoyed their love making. Mick was so gentle with her, but as each month came round her heart would sink. Gradually Mick became less and less interested in that side of things. He would be tired or some other excuse, soon love making became a thing of the past. She put up with it and got busy learning the farm work, her thrill at learning how to milk a cow, and her a city girl.

Reading in the odd magazine she bought, she read once where men can have a hormone problem affecting their prostate gland which can prevent erections, so now she knew she would never be a mother. As for Mick, he would never see a doctor and talk about that part of him, God forbid. Now a handsome young man in her bed, and at forty she was still young enough. Blessing herself and going to the little holy water font on the wall by the door, she shook some around the kitchen to get rid of the devil that's putting those thoughts into her head. Pulling off her jumper and skirt she pulled on her warm flannel nightdress, it kept her nice and warm; it was badly in need of a wash. Lying down beside Mick she couldn't help glancing across at the handsome frame facing the wall with the moonlight shining across the bed on him.

Stretching her legs across to get a feel, even if it was only his heel, it would be enough to get a thrill. All she felt was Mick's old bony ankle. Lying there staring at the window, the moonlight so splendid, could there possibly be another life out there for her. As if in answer to prayer the cow started up roaring. 'Mick, Mick, wake up, the cow is off again'. Mick forced himself out of the bed, pulled on his old jumper and trouser, picked up his old donkey jacket and headed out the door.

Now, she thought to herself, easing herself over to the middle of the bed, she could feel the heat coming from his body and the lovely American scent. Just as she was about to put her hand across his body, he turned around, lay on his side, easing himself up on his elbow he looked down on her lying there. 'Eileen' he said, 'I would love a little bit', before he could go on, she said, 'it's all yours for the taking'. He popped up on the bed, stepping over her, he headed out the bedroom door, glancing at what he was wearing in bed, it looked like a long shirt with a slit from the ankle to the knee.

She called after him, 'don't bother about locking the door Donnald, the cow will be like that for a long time yet'. Then pulling off her bloomers, she shoved it under the bolster. Donnald came back to the room with the moonlight shining on him, she could see what he had in his hand and sitting on the side of the bed he devoured the remainder of the apple cake. Eileen shoved her head under the blankets, thinking such a fool, what made me think a young man from Texas would stoop so low to satisfy a silly country woman with the smell of the cows off her. Oh God, will you forgive me ever, I must go to confession soon and confess these things I've been thinking. The apple cake finished Donnald left the black baking pan on the old chair and creeping into his side of the bed by the wall he was snoring before his head hit the bolster. Eileen pulling her head up from under the blankets rubbed the tears away.

Margaret Dowling

Bess has Twins

There wasn't a sound from the cow and no sign of Mick. What's happened, oh something bad, God is punishing me. Pulling on a scarf on her head and an old coat she ran to the cow shed, calling 'Mick, Mick, what's wrong? The cow stopped and you didn't come into the house'. Mick was sitting on an upturned butter box with the flash lamp in his hand, looking straight across in front of him. 'Mick did the cow have the calf yet'? 'Eileen, take the flash light and look for yourself'. Taking the flashlight out of his hand, she crossed over to where the cow stood. In the middle of the hay she saw a white head, 'oh! She did' and then she saw a second head that was hard to see for it was jet black. 'Mick', she yelled, 'Bess had twin calves. Oh! Mick', and rushing to him she gave him the tightest squeeze she ever could, kissing him on the cheek, 'go easy Eileen, you took the breath out of me'. 'Oh! Poor Bess, no wonder you were roaring. Had she much trouble'? 'Not with the first one with the white head, the black one, a bullock gave her a bit of trouble, but she's alright, the three of them are doing good'. 'Mick will I make you some tea'? 'No I'm going straight to bed, get some sleep. I'll need to get a can of petrol for that mans car in the morning, let him on his way, I'm sure he'll be in a hurry'. 'Have you a can Mick'? 'Yes, I left it by the bike. Alright I'll stay for a while now. The salt is there; shake a couple of fistfuls on the two of them. I'll bring in a bucket of water; the cow will need it to clean her out'.

Eileen went on her knees in the hay, prayed in thanksgiving and prayed for forgiveness. Petting and kissing Bess, 'oh you beautiful mother, twins no less'. Soon she could hear the cock crowing. 'I must leave ye now, get dressed, fix up the fire, boil the kettle, hope Mick stays in bed a while. Bye for now, happy family'. 'Moo' said the cow, getting the jobs done, grabbing the last few shillings out of a jug, she hurried out the door, picked up the can, hopped on her bike and peddled like hell to Flannery's for the petrol.

From Clare to Texas

Banging like the Devil on the door, olde Gilbert shouted 'hould your horses, do you know the hour it is'? On opening the door after pulling all the bolts, turning the key, and then lifting the latch, seeing Eileen standing there all out of breath. 'It's you Eileen at this hour, where is the fire'? 'Get busy Gilly, or there will be a fire under you, fill that can up of petrol'. 'You want petrol; sure you don't have a car'. 'No, there's a young man at the house, he lost his way last night'. 'Well be God, he must have or he wouldn't be in these parts. Did he say who he was'? 'He is over from Texas, and looking for his mother's people around here, he was talking to Mick at two o'clock this morning. Mick was up with the cow, she was in calf again'. 'You don't have to tell me, we could hear her roar all the way to here. But, tell me about the Texan, who could be around here belong to him'? 'His mother's name was Mary O'Brien from Ballygala. Would you know where that is'? 'Sure I do, that's where the old woollen mill was one time and if I know anything that little house that's the other side of the mountain is O'Brien's. The last I heard there's an old woman living on her own there'. 'That will be his aunt, is it far from our house Gilly'? 'It would be a good ten mile. But where could the Texan have stayed last night if his car ran out of petrol'? 'He stayed in our house; sure we couldn't turn him out at two o'clock in the morning. I made him tea and a piece of apple cake'. 'Your apple cake Eileen, the tastiest in the country'? 'I hope he didn't eat it all on you. Where did ye put him up'? 'He slept with Mick in the bed; I spent the night with the cow and the twin calves'. 'Twin calves did you say, well the blessing of God on you Mick Ryan. Here's the petrol that will be four shillings'. 'What four shillings after I giving news to you that you won't read in any paper'. 'Tell the Texan you paid ten for it, he won't know the difference, get it back from him. It might help towards the room and board'.

As she arrived back at the house Donnald was looking at the car, 'Eileen thank you very much'. 'You will have enough there to get you to Flannery's to fill it up. Did you have anything to eat'? Eileen enquired. 'No I didn't want to make noise. Mick, your husband seems to be in a deep sleep. He needs it the poor man. Oh! Ya, did the cow have her calf'? 'I'll let him tell you himself. I'm going to make breakfast, how many boiled eggs would you like'? asked Eileen. 'I'll take two'. 'Only two, a big man like you'? 'Yes two is good. How will I get the gas - petrol into this car'? 'Hold on I'll make you a funnel'. Going into the house she found a sheet of newspaper. Donnald was wondering did she say I'll get you a funnel, or I'll make you a funnel. 'Have you taken off the cap of the petrol tank'? 'I have' he said and to his amazement Eileen twisted the sheet of newspaper around her fingers into a perfect funnel. 'Well I never' he gasped. 'Now', she says, 'you work away and I'll get the eggs on'. What a woman, self sufficient.

Photographing the Twin Calves

She busied herself setting the table for three; she could hear Mick moving in the room. As he came out, 'Eileen, keep my eggs hot, I must get that man his petrol'. 'No need for you to do that, I already got it, and he is putting it into the car'. 'Very good Eileen, did you tell him the cow had two calves'? 'No I left that to you'.

Call him in for his breakfast now Mick. 'Good morning Donnald'. 'Good morning Mick'. 'You got the petrol into the tank alright'. 'I did, your good wife got me a can of it so it should do until I get a fill. How is the cow, did she have her calf'?

'Come down to the shed until you see'. Looking in to the cow shed it took Donnald's eyes a while to adjust to the darkness. 'Oh! Yes, a lovely little white head'. 'Look closer Donnald'. 'What! Two calves. My, good luck to them, a great cow Bess. I'm going to get my camera, this calls for photos and celebrations. Come out Mrs Ryan, I want pictures of you and Mick with ye're twin calves'. 'Oh! Great, can we have some of them pictures'? 'Sure, I'll send them to you'. He snapped this way, and that way, stand here, sit there, hold the calf's heads, it went on for ages. By the time they sat down, the breakfast was cold. Nobody seemed to care. 'Eileen said I'm naming the calves Billy and Betty'. Mick laughed, 'Oh! Woman, don't be so foolish naming calves'. 'I think it is a beautiful suggestion' put in Donnald. 'Well thanking you both very much for your hospitality and the pictures of the cow and her twins, Billy and Betty, I'll send some on to you'.

'Gilbert said you're only about ten miles from the old mill, and you might meet some one to direct you to the O'Brien's house'. Shaking hands with Donnald, she headed out to the cow shed.

Meeting Mick in the yard she asked 'Is he gone'? 'He is' said Mick, 'nice fellow'. 'Do you think so Mick? Well my opinion of him is he is one of those yanks that think they should get everything for nothing. We fed him, gave him a bed to sleep in. I took the last couple of shillings out of the jug to buy petrol for his car, maybe he thinks taking pictures of our calves with his big posh camera was thanks enough'. 'Eileen, thank God for the two healthy calves and sure what we never had we'll never miss, I know you went to a lot of trouble for him and I'm sure he wouldn't miss a pound or two, but there you are, put it out of your head now and go talk to Billy and Betty. I think we'll let them out in the field tomorrow'. Putting her arms around his neck she said 'It's along time since I said I love you, but I do'. 'Get along with yourself before you get other ideas in your head'.

Letting out the hens and doing a few jobs around the yard kept her mind off the last few hours of strange happenings. It was time to go in, wash up the breakfast delph, fix the fire, and make another apple cake and lifting the mugs and plate to put into the basin for washing. Under one plate was a folded piece of paper, she took it and opened it out. Then let out a scream, Mick heard her and came running in, 'Are you alright Eileen? What's happened'? 'Look Mick, look at this piece of paper I found under a plate'.

The Hundred Pound Note

'**S**how me'. 'It's a hundred pound note, let me sit down'. 'Eileen, you can think the wrong thing of a man'. 'I've done that a couple of times in the last few hours' she cried. 'What's that Eileen'? asked a bewildered Mick. 'Oh, nothing much'. 'How would you like to spend it Eileen'? 'Me, Mick, it's for the two of us, one thing I would like to buy is a shirt and tie for you'. 'Forget that, buy yourself a coat'. 'I will and shoes, a few things I would like for the house, I have a lot of spare time in the winter, I'm going to buy some wool and knit you a geansai, what colour would you like'? 'Oh! Eileen, a stór, don't ask me about colours. How about putting a little in the bank? How about fifty pounds, it's a long time since we went to the bank, the little bit we put in that time long ago must have a little interest on it now'. 'How did you get that thirty pounds Mick'? 'My ould bachelor uncle gave it to me on the quiet, told me put that in the bank straight away. I did, and it's there ever since. Where will we put it until we get a chance to go into Limerick'? 'What about behind one of the willow pattern plates on the dresser'. Shoving it into an old envelope Mick reached up and dropped it behind a plate. 'Now we both know where it is'. As he turned around, Eileen grabbed him around the waist and kissed him passionately. 'Eileen for heavens sake, stop that, or is it the money that has you gone astray in the head'? 'No, she thought, 'it's the twin calves. By the way Mick, you'll need to get the vet to have a look at the calves and cow'. 'You're right there Eileen and a bit of money for him too'.

'I'll have a look at the trap; it's a long time since you sat in it. We'll go a weekday, the Bank will be open. Buy what you think you need and we can bank the remainder'.

Mick set off to work outside. Before she'd make the apple cake she decided to write a list of the things needed, starting with a man's shirt and tie, some aside for the vet, ten pounds, deciding on what colour of wool to get, grey is a good colour for a man, and start on the geansai soon. I would have it made for Christmas. The list went on and on, making a guess at what each item would cost. Shirt and tie, two pounds, two shillings and sixpence, coat for herself, six pounds, maybe a head scarf, one pound, what else? Few pairs men's socks, two pounds, stockings for herself, one pound ten, shoes three pounds, a couple of pairs of bloomers for myself, that other one she shoved under the bolster, 'I must burn it as soon as I can, it gives me the shivers, mustn't think back'. Buy myself new ones, with 'his' money, she giggled. Two pound twelve shillings, some plates, mugs, new saucepan, oil cloth for the table from the market, five pounds, must tot that up, oh! The wool, we'll say three pounds. Extra groceries, another four pounds. Small bottle Paddy's, fifteen shillings, that comes to almost forty one pounds. Eileen was running away with herself thinking of what she wanted to spend the money on. 'I must stop, Mick might need a few pounds too. Well, now get on with some work, boil some water, do a wash, must be six months or more since I boiled them sheets and bolster covers. I only have the one set, sleeping on the bare thick and ould bolster, I must put it to Mick for a pair of new sheets and bolster cover. Sure he'll say 'go on Eileen, get them'. I would really need to. If one of us got sick we'd be a disgrace, need a Priest or doctor to come in. Mick, over the sixty mark now. The cow calving took a bit out of him; it's the last time he takes her to the bull'.

From Clare to Texas

Donnald on the Road Again

Driving the little car out on to the main road Donnald gave a sigh of relief. Down the road a couple of miles he got out of the car and talking to himself, 'I swear I'll never get rid of the smell of that bed, God, do they ever wash, what was I lying on and what was that long thing across the head of the bed and our three heads on it? Where will I get a bath or shower? My, the smell, it's off my clothes, it's out of the car, it's in my hair, and it's all over me. If I come across a river I swear I'll jump into it. Mom packed a towel, soap, toothpaste; I'll change out of these clothes before I meet my aunt Brid'.

After some time and driving slow lest he miss the mill. 'Ah! There it is'. Stopping and getting out, taking the camera, he pushed his way through the bushes and thorns until he was right beside the mill wheel, although overgrown with moss and weeds, the wheel was still turning slowly. The stream of water looked cool and clean, so refreshing, going back to the car he picked up his toilet bag and fresh change of clothes. Back at the stream, he thinks 'will I, or won't I'.

Bathing in the Mill River

Pulling off his clothes and stepping down into the pure clear water. Ice cold, but refreshing, not having seen a bath or shower for two days was bad enough, but that bed. Splashing and scrubbing it felt mighty good. Then something shuddered past his feet then more, what are they, yes unless I'm mistaken there is trout, fresh water trout. Leaning across the bank to reach his camera, he hoped no one would see the naked Texan in the mill river, 'now I will have some story for my mother'.

It was hard to do but he was full sure he snapped several trout. Getting out and towelling dry, his mother's towel smelled so sweet. About to dress, hearing a noise in the bushes, 'there's someone watching me' he muttered to himself. He listened, no nothing, continuing to dress, there it is again. 'Who's there, come on out of the bushes' he called. Then she appeared, with long chin whiskers. 'You startled me', she jumped down and sped past him with her two kids, but not before he got a couple of snaps of her. 'I got you, you pretty nanny goat and your twins'.

Rolling up his soiled clothes he bundled them into the trunk of the car. 'Now, I'm cleaner and fresher than I ever was in my life. Where is that cake for aunty Brid? She'll probably throw myself and it out. Where to now'? With his field glasses he could see a small house in the distance. It's the only one there, it has to be it.

Driving into the spotless swept yard he struggled out of the car, knocked on the door, which was low like Ryan's. Mustn't forget to stoop down here also. He could hear someone coming to the door with what he thought was a lame leg. Opening the door a tiny crack the old lady peeped out and asked 'Who is it'? 'Is this where Brid O'Brien lives'? asked Donnald. Opening the door back fully she reached out her hand, 'You would be my sister Mary's son'. Now it was his turn to be stunned. This was not the woman he expected to meet.

Meeting Aunt Brid

'Come on in, mind your head there, you're very tall. God bless you it's not your mother you're taking after, was your dad tall'? 'About five foot ten'. 'My, what a handsome son my sister had, and she sent you all the way here to meet me'. 'I was about to say it was my own decision. But thought better to leave the credit to mam. 'When did you land in Ireland Donnald'? 'I'm so mixed up in the days and time aunt Brid, but I think it was two days ago, I stayed in a house about ten miles from here, it was two o'clock in the morning and the car ran out of petrol right at their door, but I was in luck'. 'Here Donnald, sit by the fire, that chair there'. The chair was like a Queen Ann style chair. I sat down. 'Thank you aunty'. Aunty Brid was a welcoming woman. 'Would you like something to eat'? 'Don't go to any trouble'. 'No trouble, I could make you a fry'. 'Alright and a cup of tea'. 'Tea, Donnald, I thought you Yanks liked coffee'. 'Well, I do' Donnald shrugged. 'So I'll make you coffee then, I keep a fresh jar handy for I like it myself'. 'Well, then I'll have a mug' said Donnald agreeing with Brid.

Looking around him while she busied herself cooking, he noticed the house was shining, and around the fireplace was painted white. The floor scrubbed clean, a glass case full of glasses, with sets of every shape. A small dresser of the willow pattern in a creamy shade was up against the wall. The teapot scrubbed till you could see your face in it. Frilly lace curtains on the little window. A Sacred Heart picture supporting a small lamp with a red globe and a little light twinkling inside, hung by the chimney fire. A lovely blue flowery table cloth, all the dishes matching with blue cornflower pattern. His aunty Brid's house was like a little dolls house.

'Eat up Donnald, some more bread'? Brid asked offering Donnald a plate of bread. 'Lovely bread, your own making'? 'Yes, I never buy a loaf'. 'One minute, I must go out to the car'. Donnald brought in the cake he had for her, he hoped she would like it. 'A cake for me, thanks, what a nice thought. Now, this house you stopped at last night, who were they'? 'Well, he was elderly, she was I'd say twenty years younger. They had a cow that had twin calves, she named them Billy and Betty'. 'Yes, it sounds like the Ryan's alright'. 'That's their name alright'. 'You didn't stay the night in that house surely'? 'I did aunty; I even slept in their bed'. 'You must be walking with fleas, but you smell clean, everyone around here knows how dirty they are. Poor girl, sure she never seen how things was done. But Donnald, they don't have a bath tub'. 'Aunty, hold on to your sides, I couldn't get the smell of the place off me. The bed, well there's no describing it. So coming to the mill, I wanted to take photos of it for mom, when I seen the stream I undressed and went in'. 'You mean you washed in the mill stream in the naked'? 'I sure did'. 'Oh good God, Mary, your son'. Aunty couldn't finish her sentence with the laughing. 'I also took photos of the trout slithering along'.

'Trout, the lads at the mill used to fish a lot there. The trout is plentiful there now. I hope no-one seen my nephew in the nude'. 'Well, I did have a visitor, she hurried away with her two kids', Donnald said with a grin on his face, 'a nanny goat! I got a good photo of her racing away'. 'What did you do with your dirty clothes'? 'I put them in the car trunk'. 'Trunk Donnald, you didn't go bringing a trunk'? 'No aunty, I mean the boot of the car'. 'Are they still in it'? 'They are'. Soon as you are finished eating, take them out and throw them in that heap over there, it's where I put stuff to burn, do you mind doing that'? 'Thanks a million aunty, I'll do it right now'. Opening the boot of the car, the smell hit him in the face. 'Thanks aunty, I'd better leave it open for a while'. 'I can't believe you slept in that house. Whatever possessed her to marry an old man? She must have been quite a looker in her young days'.

Aunty gives Eileen's History

The story flows like this. 'Poor Eileen worked in her father's pub in Limerick. The bar was one end and the grocery to the other end. She worked very long hours serving them, the old men coming in at any hour. Still, he kept her on her feet; all he cared about was the money they took in. No regard for his daughter. His wife had four other children, and the youngest was a son. The second oldest, a little retarded girl, then two other younger daughters. Well, it seems Mick Ryan used to go into the grocers to get his messages, and then went down to the bar for his pint, like most of the customers did the same thing. Somehow Eileen got talking to Mick and through time she was talking to him more and more and slipping him the odd free pint.

She would come from behind the bar to fix the fire at the end of the shop, and Mick would be sitting on a stool at the fire sipping his pint. It was an excuse to fix the fire and have a little hand holding, that was all it was 'hand holding'. She would take that chance when the father would be gone out the back to bring in a barrel of Guinness. Sure, some of the boys up at the bar were watching all this. Maybe an odd one jealous, for Eileen was a pretty girl with a touch for pulling a good pint. One evening the father caught the two holding hands, well he hit poor Mick such a clout, and he nearly broke his jaw. Cleared him from the public house entirely.

Embarrassing poor Eileen, she was crying her heart out. 'Get there and serve the customers, you hussy. Ah now Donnald, it was a shocking thing for any father to do, to his daughter and she slaving in his bar from she was sixteen years old. And, she now almost twenty one. I don't think she was ever at a dance or any sort of enjoyment'. 'But Aunty, they seemed to have come close together'.

The Plan

'They did and I'll tell you how. The grocery end of that premises was belonging to her father's brother, George Downs, her dads name was Chris Downs. Well, Mick kept coming in to see George for his little bag of groceries; of course he had to turn his back on the pub. Shortly after the upset, George met Eileen as she was getting a few items of groceries for her mother. In a whisper he says 'if you want any messages passed to Mick, leave it with me'. She grabbed her chance. A note soon was passed saying 'Mick meet me Saturday night at about ten o'clock down at the old forge, have a spare bike with you if you can'. As George took the note he passed her a five pounds note, a gift from your old Uncle George. 'Thank you George'. Eileen knew Saturday nights were the busiest in the pub; she would pretend to be feeling sick. Pack a little bag and make a run for it. She prayed it would be one of them dark misty nights.

When George passed the note to Mick with his change, Mick looked in his hand, and George said in a hushed tone, 'a message for you'. Mick rushed on home, trying to think where he could get a ladies bike for the night, and then he thought of Gilbert Flannery. Gilbert would give him his wife's bike flying, without a question. 'Thanks Gill, I'll have it back in a couple of hours', 'no hurry Mick'.

Poor Eileen was sneaking around in search of a small bag, she didn't have much to pack, the few shillings her dad gave her, when he did give it, wouldn't buy her a pair of stockings. 'What happened then aunty'?

'Well, she was up in the room she shared with the sister that's not too well, picking out things to shove into the bag, she could hear her dad shouting at her mother, 'get Eileen out here, the pub is getting very busy now'. 'Eileen is feeling sick'. 'She's what? Go out there, keep an eye on things, I'll see how sick she is'. Eileen could hear him pounding up the stairs; she threw the bag on the bed and lay down on the top of it. 'What's with you? Don't you know you are needed in the pub on a busy Saturday night'? 'My head is very dizzy'. 'Did you take anything for it'? 'Mam gave me two tablets but they make you very drowsy'.

Aunty tells of the Escape

'Well, you better stay there then, can't have you confusing the change. Your mother will have to do, she's not much good at it, but she'll be better than nothing. Be down at ten in the morning to clean up'. 'I will dad'. Thanking God to herself she wasn't caught. The night was very dark, it was after ten o'clock, and she hoped Mick would wait for her. She would need to go very easy, slip out the back door and pray her father wouldn't be there bringing in the porter. Mustn't draw attention to herself. There were a lot of bikes lying about, 'a fair crowd of the lads in tonight' she said to herself. My poor mother, he'll go pure mad in the morning. It will give Mick and myself plenty of time to escape. These were her thoughts, Donnald, and she on her way. 'Go on aunty', he pressed.

'Mick was there, he eased the bikes out of the darkness of the forge, hop on quick Eileen, and we can talk later. No doubt Mick was in love with her, but she was only twenty one. Twenty years younger than Mick. Well Donnald, the two poor creatures cycled as fast as they could out that road until they arrived at Flannery's Garage. Mick slipped the borrowed bike into the garage, noticing that the house was in darkness, Mick remarked it must be after midnight. That family never go to bed before twelve o'clock. Feeling relaxed for the time been, they walked slowly the six miles to Mick's house. Safely back in Mick's little house, Eileen felt tired but relaxed for some strange reason. She had no fear in her. 'I have something to tell you now Eileen, after I got your note from George, the first thing I did, I went to the bus station and bought two return tickets to Dublin for tomorrow, Sunday morning, bright and early'. 'Why did you do that Mick'? Eileen asked. 'I'll tell you why and I hope you are in agreement. About a year ago I met an ould fellow at a fair I was at, trying to sell a couple of head of cattle. We struck up a conversation during the course of it. The ould fellow told me of a priest in Dublin who will marry anyone providing they are of age, twenty one or over, and he won't ask too many questions. But you can't be married to anyone else. He even gave me the priest's name and address; I still have that piece of paper rolled up and stuck in an old jug, never thinking I would have the courage to put it to my own use. Then down he went on one knee, saying I'm not much at romantic speech'.

Mick Proposes

'**I**'m asking you dear Eileen, to marry me. I don't have an engagement ring but I have my mothers, may she rest in peace, wedding ring, and if your answer is yes, it will make me very happy and I'll do what I can for you for the rest of my life'. After that little speech, Eileen was overcome, putting her arms around his neck. 'No Eileen', says Mick 'what's your answer'. 'Mick', says she, 'I hope that priest is there tomorrow, I will indeed marry you Mick'. Giving her a little kiss, he thanked her. 'Now Eileen', he says, 'what age are you'? 'I'm over twenty one'. 'Have you your birth certificate with you'? 'I have Mick, I have everything I own in that little bag, I don't want for any reason to go back near that house again, but I know I'll miss mam and my poor handicapped sister'.

'Don't fret a stór, you will see them again. I know this isn't much of a place to bring a nice girl like you into, but we will do it up a bit, a lick of white wash on the walls, a bit of paint on the door and windows and sure you'll have a palace'.

This made Eileen giggle. 'I'll make us two hot toddies; you have been pouring drinks for long enough, now I'll do it'. That gave them a laugh. 'I've the bed fixed up for you and I'll settle in front of the fire myself, get a bit of sleep, we won't have very long. I've the alarm clock set for five, we would need to be out of here before six. We don't want to miss the bus. If there's no-one waiting at the end of the road at seven he just speeds past. We will need to stand well out so he can see us. It will be dark'. Another kiss and then two hours sleep. I tell you Donnald, sleep didn't bother either of them'. 'Come on, come on aunty, keep telling it' begged Donnald.

'They got the bus, no other passengers on it, only themselves for miles and anyone that got on wouldn't have known them. 'Mick' she says, 'do you think we will have enough money'? 'I've return tickets, we'll have enough for a couple of meals, have you much money'? 'I've twenty pounds. And, I've ten pounds; five Uncle George gave me, poor Uncle George, and five in change.

That should cover the Priest, maybe we'll have to pay witnesses, the ould fellow that told me about this, and said the Priest's housekeeper and husband usually takes a pound. But if its strangers they won't take anything'.

Mick and Eileen arrive in Dublin

'Well Donnald, with shaking knees, they knocked at the Priest's door. Mick turned to Eileen and said 'I bet he is out saying Mass'. The housekeeper opened the door, a cheerful Dublin woman. 'Come in' she says, 'I'll tell Father Kenny you're here'. They sat down in the waiting room. Father Kenny came in, they went to stand up, 'sit, sit, now my good people getting married is it'? 'Yes' they both chorused! 'Names please and address'. Mick gave that. 'Now there's only one reason I can't marry a couple and that is if they're under age. Now, Eileen Downes you only look eighteen to me'. 'I'm twenty one Father'. 'Have you proof'? 'I have my birth certificate Father with me'. 'Show me, yes, that's in order. Well Mick and Eileen, I'm going in just now to St Agnes to say Mass, so go ahead in, sit in the front seat and we'll make a very special occasion out of this Blessed event. I'll marry you during the Mass, would you like that'? 'Yes, Father'. 'Very good, we'll call a couple of witness's from the congregation to stand for ye, alright'? 'Thank you Father. Stay there, I want to have a word with the housekeeper'. Eileen was both happy and nervous. 'Now, my good people, after your wedding you can both come back here as Mr and Mrs Ryan and join me for Breakfast'. Mick stood up and in a bit of a low voice he said 'Father, we don't have much money, can you tell me what you charge for the marriage and breakfast and I'll pay you now, here Father, will ten pounds do'? 'Put your money into your pocket, you will be needing it'.

Mass was lovely, the two of them sitting in the front seat with two strangers. When the Priest called them to the altar the two strangers went up as well, Eileen thinking to herself, there must be four getting married at the one time. Before Father Kenny went on with the ceremony he turned to Eileen and said, 'This is your bridesmaid Peg, and Michael this is Dan your bestman. Pass him the ring and he will hand it back to you at the time for you both to become husband and wife'. Mick was so nervous he could hardly find the ring down in the corner of his pocket wrapped in a piece of brown paper.'

'Well, they were married and the congregation gave a big clap, sure God help us I don't think they knew what was happening. After the Mass, like the Priest told them to, they went to his house. 'Now, Mr and Mrs Ryan', says the Priest, 'you're heartily welcome to have breakfast with me and my friends'. The spread that was laid on that table, you wouldn't see in any big hotel, the two of themselves, the housekeeper and her husband, the two witnesses and two other friends, plus the Priest. They drank and they feasted until they were ready to burst. Dan, the best man, proposed a toast to the bride and groom. The housekeeper had a lovely little cake prepared. 'Now Mr and Mrs Ryan, cut your wedding cake'. Poor Eileen was so overcome, she cried.

Wedding Breakfast and Gifts

When they were leaving, for they had to catch a bus back to Ballygala, Father Kenny says to his housekeeper, 'fill a bag of what is left over for these good people'. 'Indeed I will Father, now there's a bag of the finest food for the two of ye and I've put in a pot of my homemade apple jam'. The two couples handed them ten pounds each. Twenty pounds in all. 'Have a happy life and good luck to you both Mr and Mrs Ryan'. Looking at Mick, Eileen says, 'I'm Mrs Mick Ryan now'. 'You are, did you enjoy all that fussing this morning'? 'I did, husband'. 'Go on with you wife', smiled Mick. The bag was heavy; Eileen didn't see what the Priests housekeeper put into it. She hoped for a piece of the cake.

'Well Donnald, things were done in strange ways back then. Men as young as lads were kept working on the land. There was little time for courting a young girl. So the chance of marriage passed them by and they died lonely old bachelors, God help us. There were matchmakers who were sometimes lucky in bringing two together, but that's another story'. 'So aunty, how did her father take this kind of marriage for his daughter, I'm sure the news got around'? 'Wait till you hear what he did to the poor girl'. 'Yes, tell me' (Donnald at this time is sitting on the edge of his chair, a hand on each knee, his mouth open, looking into his aunts face. Brid of course, relishing in the listeners interest in her story, continued). 'Mick and Eileen were only home a couple of days, Eileen busy in the kitchen making an apple cake, which she was very good at. On hearing a van drive into the yard, and on looking out the window, she saw her father coming out of the van.

Eileen's Dad in a Rage

And he roaring out of his belly, 'Out, come out here Eileen Downes, no daughter of mine is going to shack up in a pigsty like this'. Eileen was shaking in her shoes, poor thing. Then she saw Mick coming toward her dad, the dung fork in his hand, aimed at Chris, her dad. 'Get off my land Chris Downes, Eileen is no longer your daughter, but my wife'. 'You dirty ould man, tell me another one'.

'Get off my land or I'll run you through'. 'Not until I see proof of what you just said.' Eileen was inside the window she stuck up her left hand with the ring on her finger. 'That's not going to satisfy me, I want to see written proof'. Lucky enough the Priest had given them a Church Marriage Certificate, so she brought that to the window and stuck it up for the dad to see.

'You'll be sorry, Mick Ryan for bringing my daughter into filth like this, you haven't heard the last of this yet'. 'She came willingly and anything, even this filth as you call it, is better than the kind of life you gave her'. The shouts and roars of the two men could be heard all over the Parish. Her father roared away in his van, nearly knocking Mick down. Going into the house to see if Eileen was alright, he found her cowering in the bedroom, 'Come out Eileen a grá, that ould father of yours is full of hot air'. 'Oh! Mick, I'm so frightened'. 'Don't be now a girl. Make a pot of tea for the two of us and sure we might finish off your wedding cake'. 'I will Mick' she says and busied herself. 'But aunty, I must ask you this, how did you find out all the information as to how it all came about, how she ran away from her home, running off with this man to get married and so on'? 'Your mother, my sister, sent me some lovely wool around that time. The colours were splendid, the likes couldn't be got here anywhere. I knitted up a lot of garments, mixing colours and so on, I would cycle into Limerick of a Saturday to sell, go around the shops (stores) as you say, leave some scarf's and hats into the shopkeepers, some of my knitting at times would be bought there and then, the rest

I would leave for a couple of weeks. After I was finished that business, I would head to Downes Grocers to buy my few messages. Sometimes, but only sometimes, I would go to the bar at the end of the premises, sit by the fire for a while sipping my glass of port wine and listen to the gossipers. I tell you Donnald, you would get an education. The whole conversation was about Eileen and poor ould Mick, and all in whispered tones, indeed from beginning to end the gossipers knew it all. Eileen used to meet her Uncle George; no doubt he was good to her, slipping her the odd few pounds of tea, sugar, salt and the like. Sure she would confide her troubles in him and of course it wouldn't stop there. George would relay the story to his wife, from there it would spread. Ah! Sure Donnald, the people around here had nothing much for doing. So any bit of gossip would be well trashed out for weeks. Now her Dad didn't let it rest there'.

Then the Guards came

A week or so after the big uproar, Mick and Eileen were sitting by the fire drinking their hot cocoa, it was late, and they weren't expecting anyone. A car drove into the yard. Poor Eileen took a run for the room, and cocoa mug went too, the lot went flying into the fire. Inside in that room, poor Eileen was shaking. A big knock at the door. Mick opened it, Mick wasn't afraid of anything. What was standing there, but two policemen. 'Mick Ryan we have a serious complaint about you threatening Chris Downes who came to speak to his daughter. We believe she is here against her will, where is she now'? 'She's back in the bedroom'. 'Oh! We see', says the two police men, eyeing each other. 'Is there a chance we could speak to this girl'? 'Of course', says Mick. To this day I'm sure Mick still doesn't know how he thought of it, but going to the bedroom door he says 'Mrs Ryan, there's two police men here wants to see you , bring that certificate with you'. The two police men took a different kind of look at each other. 'Mrs Ryan, ye're husband and wife'? 'We are that', 'show them the marriage cert'. 'That's in order. Did your father give you permission Mrs Ryan? You must be only about eighteen'? 'Go and get the other cert Eileen' Mick said to Eileen. She showed them the Birth Cert. 'Yes, you are of age. That's alright Mrs Ryan'.

'Now Mick you threatened Mr Downes with a heavy fork'. 'I told that man to get off my land and leave my wife alone, and like with ye we had to prove we were legally married to him'. 'Why did you have the fork in your hand coming towards him'? 'I'm a farmer, that morning I was filling the wheelbarrows with manure to take down to the garden to spread where I was going to plant potatoes'. 'So you had legal reason for holding the fork'? 'Yes Sir, I did'. 'All right Mick we won't trouble you any more, neither will Mr Downes. Good night Mrs Ryan'. Well Donnald, no word of a lie whatever the guards said to Chris Downes he never did a bit of good after that night, took to the drink, drank himself into the grave. It was Eileen, what she did, took him down a peg or two. 'Whatever happened to his pub' asked Donnald. 'I told you Eileen had two younger sisters, well gradually as he was going into decline they would work the bar, even though they were still very young. They're married now with children and their husbands work the bar. Their mother, God rest her, when Chris wasn't too well she used to take the child that wasn't too well and they'd sit at the shop fire, the gossip would stop and she knew when she would sit. There were certain old women coming in there for the sheer purpose of scandal mongering. 'What happened to the son Brid'? 'Chris junior never set foot in the bar, the plans were, or so rumour had it, that he was to get the pub, lock stock and barrel. He is a big solicitor now down in Cork. 'And the groceries, is that still there'?

'Oh yes, George's family are running that'. 'Aunty couldn't we go there and have a drink, I feel I would like to drink to Mick and Eileen. I'm very glad I did what I did'.

Donnald's Explanation

'Donnald, what did you do'? 'For their trouble Brid'. 'Trouble yes', Brid laughs. 'Stop aunty, for a stranger like me they gave such hospitality too, they have big hearts'. 'Tell me what you did Donnald'? 'On leaving I was going to leave them a twenty pound note under a plate on the table, but all I had was a ten and a hundred, so I left the hundred pounds'. 'Well that must have been the most money they ever saw in their lives, God will bless you for it. You will stay the night? 'I will aunty'. 'Good, I'll pull out the folding bed and I'll sleep on it, you're a big fellow and need the bed'. 'Now aunty, if I'm going to put you out of your bed I won't stay'. 'Here, help me with this; do you think you would fit in that'? 'Aunty, look at the car outside, the size of a match box, when I can fit in that I'll fit in anything. I would like to visit the grandparent's grave soon'. 'Sure Donnald, I'll take you down there now. Just wait and I'll fix the piece of bacon and cabbage for our dinner'. 'We're having bacon and cabbage'? 'You don't like that'? 'Sure, I love it, but it was the last meal mom and I had together before I left Texas'. 'My God, can you believe that'!

From Clare to Texas

Eileen's Spending Spree

Eileen felt like a queen sitting in the pony and trap heading into Limerick. Looking across at Mick she said 'wasn't it very strange how you hid that hundred pound note behind the same willow pattern plate where you hid the marriage cert and my birth cert years ago'. 'I was thinking that same thing mysel', sure it's over twenty years ago since all that happened'. 'Yes Mick do you remember our wedding day, wasn't he a lovely Priest'. 'He was indeed Eileen'. Poor Mick, so nice to her all them years. 'I have had two outstanding days in my life that I've enjoyed, my wedding day and today going to spend these hundred pounds. I can just picture myself in a lovely red coat and a pretty scarf strutting down through the church on Sunday. Where did she get the price of that from now? I can hear the jealous ould biddies saying. Maybe from that fellow that lost his way. Well they'd be right there'. Sitting in the trap and looking out over the pony's head. Mick couldn't help noticing the smile on her lips. Poor Eileen it was easy to keep her happy, such a shame they had no children, she would have made a great mother, my fault, the feeling went off me long ago, I suppose I should have gone to a doctor about it, but how could a man like me talk about that part of me to even a doctor. Eileen accepted it in the end. She has given me a few funny kind of hugs lately, sure that sort of feeling couldn't be on her now at forty one years of age?

'First thing Eileen, we'll go to the bank, I've my bank book here, after all the years its time I put your name to it'. 'What will we save Mick'? 'Put in thirty, at least that's something, you'll need it as a little nest egg. You have a lot to buy, it's a good idea to get sheets and a bolster cover, now for some money spending, go ahead on your own, and I'm going to look for cabbage plants, onion sets and potato seeds. I hope there is enough room in the trap to take home all you buy' he laughed. After a few hours of shopping, then meeting Mick, he enquired 'did you get everything you needed'? 'Everything, but the groceries Mick'.

Revisiting the Pub

It's a long time since I set foot in the pub I used to work and live in. 'Do you think I would have the courage to go in there now Mick'? 'Why wouldn't you, I'll be with you. Your sisters will be happy to see you; if they're not then they will have to answer to me. Alright, go and get the groceries, meet your cousins and we will have a drink in the bar where we met. I wonder if the fireplace is still there'. They laughed together at that memory. Getting the few messages, chatting to the cousins, Eileen asked if her sisters were working in the bar. 'Yes', they told her, 'go on in there and talk to them'.

Turning to approach the bar, something caught her eye, 'Mick' she says, 'look, do you see that man talking to the old woman, the one with his back to us'? 'Yes, what about him'? 'I could be mistaken, but I would swear its Donnald'. 'Be gob, your right Eileen. We'll go and say hello to them, the old woman must be the aunt he was looking for. Come on Eileen, look at me, the ould coat I've on'. 'You're alright, your hair is nice'. 'I got it cut, and a shampoo and blow dried'. 'My Eileen, but you're using words I never heard you use before', smiled Mick. 'Hello Donnald, it is Donnald'? 'Why Mick Ryan and your good wife, I'm so happy to meet you again. This is Aunty Brid. Pleased to meet you both. I was just saying to aunty how I would like to drink a toast to Mick and his wife in Downes bar, so she showed me how to get here. I'm staying a couple of days with her before I travel north. Please sit down, what will you have'? 'I'll have a bottle of stout' Mick answered. 'And you, Mrs Ryan'? 'I'll have a sherry' said Eileen. 'Very good, I'm glad of this opportunity'. Up at the bar Donnald was not a man to mince his words, in his loud Texan drawl. While they were pouring the drink Eileen could hear him saying, 'see that lady sitting at the fire, she used to work in this bar, serving up drink, just as you are doing now'. The older of the two women stared over at Eileen. 'My God, it's my sister Eileen'. With the shock of it, Kate dropped the glass, bottle and all. 'Hello Kate', says Eileen. 'I didn't know you Eileen for a minute, your hair is different'. 'I had it done today'. 'It suits you'. Then turning to Rita she says, 'Rita look over at the fire, that's our sister Eileen'. Running across the floor the two of them almost knocked each other over trying to be first to kiss and hug Eileen. 'It's years', 'It is ten, that's how long our mother is dead. Poor mom, she was a good mother, but I could never come near the house to see her, not while my stupid father was in it'. 'He gave you a hard life of it'. 'He did, five hard years I slaved for him, but I think I would at that time have forgiven him only for the blow he hit Mick and then barring him from the bar'. 'You got your own back on him Eileen'. 'Even then he couldn't leave me alone. And then sending two guards to our home and nearly arrested Mick'. 'What happened after that? Kate, how did he turn to the drink, what did the Guards say to him'? 'I don't think it was anything to do with the guards' answered Kate looking away into the distance.

Dad took to the Bottle

'That night when they came back after been to ye're place he was watchin' out the window to see their car driving in. He ran to open the door, sure there was only the two of them there, the first words he said was, 'Where is she'? 'I told ye not to come without her' said an annoyed Chris. 'Whether you like it Chris or not they're husband and wife and no-one can interfere there'. 'Are ye not arresting him for threatening me with the dung fork'? 'No the man was doing his days work and had a genuine reason to have it in his hand. You shouldn't have gone into his property in the temper you were in. Maybe if you had treated your daughter right it would never have happened. You have two other daughters there Chris; don't do the same to them'.

'From then on he took to the drink. Mammy would send the two of us out to serve in the bar, and sure we did our best. He wouldn't look at us; and then gradually the business went into decline. Mammy got sick and sure the two of us there trying to look after her, and looking at him lying in a chair from morning till night with the bottle in his hand. Our poor sister, Sissy, getting more confused every day. Eventually the doctor signed her into a home and she's still there. Rita and myself take it in turns to take her out at the weekends. When poor mam passed away we seen you at the funeral, we couldn't bring ourselves to talk to you, the loss of our good mother, and yours too. When we did go looking for you there was no sign of you. We had seen you again a month later when daddy passed away. This time we didn't go to speak to you, we felt there was anger in you and rightly so'. 'It's all out of me now Kate; I want to tell you who helped me escape that night long ago'. 'Who Eileen'? 'It was mam, God rest her, she said, go and may God go with you. I said mam, what about you when he finds out in the morning. I'll deal with that, she said. What do you know Rita, didn't our mam have courage'. 'We won't upset you now with what happened that morning, the things he said to her, oh, she was no good. He said things like you and your retard kid. Poor Sissy, it's hard to know if poor Sissy understood'.

'You married Mick, are you happy Eileen'? 'I am, very happy. There's no-one shouting at me, or working me to the bone. But I work a lot outdoors and I work hard. You got married too Kate'. 'Yes, I'm Mrs Frank McGovern now'. 'They wouldn't be the McGovern's out on the Fursey Road with the big farm and three or four hay barns, tractors and the devil knows what, how did you chance to snare one of them'? Eileen enquired.

Eileen hears about her Sisters Marriages'

Coming into the pub and sitting by the fire, holding hands with each other 'Come on Kate stop, you're making fun of me'. 'I'm only joking Eileen, our mother used to tell us about you and Mick holding hands at the fire. But, sure that was how I met Frank, coming in on a Saturday night. Then he started asking me out, and we got married fourteen years ago, Frank Óg is now thirteen. We have four kids; the youngest is eight year old Kathleen'. 'My, Mrs McGovern, what about you Rita'? 'What Mrs are you? Oh! Wisha, I'm Mrs Tom Egan, met him through the pub also, we have no family and we won't, I've some sort of growths that's stopping me getting pregnant, I've had more operations than I have fingers and toes'. 'What about young Chris?' 'He is a solicitor, married a doctor, Lisa Moran, they're living in Cork, with their two sons'. 'Well indeed, I wasn't invited to any of your weddings' remarked Eileen. A long silence - then Rita put her arm around her shoulders, 'you didn't invite us to yours'. Eileen lets out a big laugh. 'My God 'mine', that's a story and a half. But it was the happiest day of my life'.

'Wait a minute', says Kate, 'while we're talking here we could be in the kitchen eating and drinking. Come on Eileen, yourself and Mick and sure Donnald and his aunt are welcome in too'. 'Thanks Kate, but the cow had twin calves a few days ago and we need to get back to them'. 'Twin calves Eileen, I never seen twin calves'. 'Well, you're both welcome out to see them anytime'. 'Thanks Eileen, we will do that, but first we must arrange a get together, for all of us, Chris junior and family too. You must tell us all about your wedding day'. 'We will and thanks Kate and Rita, we will see ye soon'. 'Alright Eileen and Mick, you did a big shop there, did you buy out the town'? Eileen laughed as they went out the door.

Looking at Eileen, Donnald asked 'How are ye travelling'? Pony and trap Donnald'. 'Pony and trap, where are they'? 'Come on' says Mick, 'I'll show you'. Eileen shouts 'Donnald, have you got your camera with you'?

Donnald takes more Photos

'**Y**es I do, I want pictures of you in the trap'. 'Oh! Mick, how quaint is that, we have many buggies in Texas, but nothing like this'. Donnald walked around and around the pony and trap taking pictures this side, that side, get into it, 'can you really fit all them parcels in it'? 'We can indeed, thanks Donnald. And thanks Donnald for the money, only for it we would have none of these parcels'. 'No, no, thank you for helping me out that night. Now aunty, stand next the trap and I'll take one last shot. That is beautiful. Bye for now Mr and Mrs Ryan'.

On the way home all the parcels on the floor and upon the seats, there was just enough room for the two of them to sit. 'Sure, you had to tell them about the calves. You are mad about them twin calves'. 'I am Mick, they're my babies, I mean our babies'. (An awkward moment passed).

'Why didn't you go into the kitchen when Kate asked you too'? 'I couldn't, I'm just not ready for that yet. Mam isn't there and my clothes, these ould things I'm wearing, well, I just wouldn't feel comfortable. When I get myself sorted out and dress in my new blue coat and scarf and shoes, then I'll strut my stuff and you'll strut yours in the new grey geansai I'll knit you, and then we will go together into that kitchen'. The two of them laughed about that. 'Mick, today is another one of my happiest days, I've met my sisters again. I never thought they would even be bothered with me'. 'Why in the world wouldn't they?' 'You did nothing to them Eileen. While you were talking to Kate, Rita was telling me that Kate and the family are living about two miles from the pub. Rita and Tom live in the old house. They made a lot of renovations to it. The husbands take turns working the pub, and use the kitchen for grubbing up'. 'You got that news good there. Mick I hope our little calves Billy and Betty will be there when we arrive home. No-one will touch them in broad day light, will they'? 'They're well locked in, and ould Rover is in the yard'. 'Yes our guard dog'. Rover gave them a big welcome, giving them a wag of his tail as the trap pulled into the yard. Mick's priority was to give the calves freedom, and watch them gallop off down the field.

'Look out there Eileen, what do you see? Billy and Betty enjoying they're freedom'. 'I'll help you in with the parcels as soon as I leave the plants and seeds into the shed'. Eileen gathered up all she could take into the house. There was so much she didn't think at the time, that she had bought so much. She decided to leave the groceries for Mick to take in. The fire had to be set and lit to boil the kettle and a dinner to be made. Lamb chops, when did they last have lamb chops for dinner? Mick carried in the bags of groceries. As he left them down Eileen turned to him, 'wasn't it a good day Mick'? 'It was Eileen, you met your sisters', 'I did and Donnald and the aunt, and the shopping, Oh!, it was a great day' she said and flinging her arms around his neck, she held him tight, kissing him, 'I sure love you Mick'. 'Eileen act your age girl'. 'I am, we have let too much time pass and not enough loving'. 'I can love you without all the clinging stuff'. She laughed at that. 'While the dinner is boiling I'll open the things out of the parcels. We can look at them after dinner'. Mick went out to do some jobs. Thinking what's coming over that woman?

Setting out the table nicely Eileen placed the new plates and mugs gently on the new oil cloth. Trying to get the delph to match the flowers in the tablecloth, she complimented herself on her own tasty choice.

Calling Mick to his dinner, they both sat into the pretty laid out table. Home grown potatoes, vegetables and the lamb chops, she watched Mick nosh his chop, holding it in his two hands. Grease up to his two ears, then wiping his fingers in the front of his old, already dirty shirt. She was in too happy a mood to make a comment.

'Any money left after your big shopping spree Eileen'? 'About twelve pounds'. 'I'm getting the vet tomorrow Eileen, let him have a look at the calves'. 'Oh yes, I must leave some money out for him. Have you ever met Donnalds aunt Brid before today'? 'I knew about herself and her sister, Donnalds mother, around these parts you might get to meet the odd one at the ceili, the sisters would be older than me. How old is Brid'? 'I think around the seventy's'. 'She looks more'. 'There's no ceili's now, the old school is closed up, a lot of people from Ballygala either left or died, very few new people coming here now, not much for them, the land is poor quality'. 'Your bit of land seems to be fairly good Mick'? 'I keep tilling it and changing where to plant potatoes and so on, plenty of manure that's the tip. I'll go out and take a look where I'll put the cabbage plants and seed potatoes this year'. 'And I'll wash up' said Eileen gathering up the delph. 'I'm glad I thought of getting knitting needles and a knitting pattern. I'll enjoy making this geansai; sure I was a good knitter in school. Lovely grey wool with black fleck. Put up the stitch, and make a start'.

Passion

At the end of that happy day bed was a welcome sight. As they lay down Eileen wrapped her arms around her husband. 'Eileen, a grá, no more squeezing'. Mick wasn't ready for the excitement in Eileen. It was more than a hug she was looking for, kissing him passionately, her tender warm body pressed to his. He was overcome with an emotion he never before felt in his existence.

Relaxing, they both fell asleep. Slipping out of bed Eileen looked out the little window, the sun was shining on the cobble stones, what a lovely day. I must let the geese and fowl out in it. Thinking at the same time she would make Mick a pot of stirabout. She could hear the sound of the milk hitting the side of the bucket. It was like music to her ears; the fresh milk continued to fill the buckets with the strength of his hands. Preparing breakfast she hummed a tune to herself. Mick brought in the two flowing buckets of milk and placed them on the kitchen floor, steam rising from the thick froth. Tabby, the cat roused himself from in front of the fire, stood waiting for his saucer of the warm milk. 'There Eileen, you'll have to strain and separate the milk today, I'm not feeling too well'. 'What is it Mick'? gasped Eileen.

'It's me heart Eileen, it's beating so fast it feels as if it's going to tear out of my chest'. 'Come Mick, I'll help you into bed and I'll get the doctor'. 'After a lie down I'll be fine'. 'Mick dear, you're working away too hard'. 'The work didn't do it to me Eileen'. 'What then Mick'? 'You and your passion last night'. 'Oh! Mick that little bit of loving, could it have brought on a heart attack'? 'Eileen I'm not fit, so no more of it now'. 'I was going to make a pot of stirabout, would you like that'? 'Yes, and leave it there, I'll eat it later'. 'I'm sorry Mick', she started to cry, 'I never meant to bring a heart attack on you'. 'It's alright, I'll rest and be as good as new. Go on with your work and forget about this now'. 'I'll strain and separate the milk, let out the cows and feed the calves'. Going about her work Eileen couldn't help worrying about Mick. I'll check on him in a while. I have never seen him take a day in bed before. Dear God, I didn't buy new sheets to put them to use this soon. Tiptoeing into the bedroom, she could hear Mick sleeping peacefully. Placing her hand on his chest she could feel the gentle beat of his heart. Thanking God that the crisis had passed now, Eileen she said to herself, 'you will keep your passionate feelings under control in future'. Relaxing and doing some knitting, Eileen was feeling better herself.

Eileen in Charge

Feeling pleased with herself being in charge of the farm stock when the vet came. 'Good woman yourself', said the vet 'your calves are good healthy beasts. They will bring a good price when Mick takes them to the next fair'. 'They're not for sale; they're my babies' answered Eileen with a laugh. 'Mick will have his own ideas on that one' said the vet. 'What do I owe you Mr Brown'? 'Six pounds, I won't charge you for my call out, just for the injections will do'. 'Thank you', 'my regards to Mick'.

Next morning Mick was his old self again walking around the farm and looking at the stock. Eileen was happy about that, but kept avoiding him, feeling embarrassed. Why should I be embarrassed she thought, isn't that what married people do, oh I can't look him in the face.

Over dinner Mick broke the silence. 'How's my geansai coming on'? 'I'll show it to you, I should have it finished for Christmas. Do you like the colour Mick'? Only Mick did not answer her question, instead he said 'you're a good and handsome young woman; I should never have married you, an ould codger like me. You weren't in love with me; it was an escape for you from your ould father'. 'I will be honest with you Mick, it wasn't love, but deep down I liked your kind and easy way of going. I've built up a great respect and love for you over the years Mick. I could never give you what you really deserve'.

Mick reveals his Background

'Look at what you walked into and have lived in ever since, filth and clobber, it was true for your dad, God Rest his Soul, what he said'. 'I love you and I will until I die Mick'. 'A kinder heart there never was. I have never known much about being neat and clean myself, my poor mother died a few days after I was born. My dad reared me the first two years of my life. He got pneumonia and died, his brother Danny brought me up here, a kind ould soul. I wasn't in school much, the school guards came a few turns, threatened to have me taken away. By the time I was fourteen they couldn't touch me. A couple of good neighbouring women seen to it that I was dressed and made my first Communion and my Confirmation. Father Clancy was a man who would leave no-one out. He advised ould uncle Danny to Will this place to me, so I would have a home to live in. When the two of us were in good working form this place was in better condition'. 'So that's your background Mick'. 'It is, most of it anyway'. 'At the same time, Mick I think you should see a doctor'. 'It's a bit late in life for to have that part of me examined'. 'I mean your heart Mick; you shouldn't have had such a strong palpitation'. 'I'm sure you're right, Eileen, and I will see him the first chance I have'. 'Do you need my help outside'?

'No Eileen, I know you are itching to be getting on with the knitting. Well the sooner the geansai is made the sooner you can wear it'.

Donnald meets Father Tomson

'It's getting on in the evening aunty; do you think the little Chapel is open? We could pay a visit there'. 'Yes Donnald and you can snap more photos for your mother'. 'You know me already aunty'. 'I think I know you all your life Donnald'.

'Thanks for the kind welcome you gave me when you reached out your welcoming arm'. I was surprised aunty you did that. And aunty, by way of repayment I'm bringing you back to Texas and get you a new hip, you won't have any more pain, you would like that aunty'? 'I would but I'm too old for a journey like that. I would only be a burden to you and my sister, Mary whom I haven't spoken too in years'. 'All I ask of you Aunty is to write a letter to mam, express your feelings to her. I will post it on my way up North'. 'I will take a chance with getting you a passport in the Irish Passport Office in Dublin; I can take the necessary certificates with me and a letter from the cops'. 'Cops Donnald'? 'Garda, I meant to say'.

'Don't put yourself out for me Donnald; I'm overcome with joy that my sister sent her son all this way to see me'. Again Donnald was tempted to say it was his own idea, but no this was going too good now. Aunty was about to write a letter asking mom to pardon her for the years wasted. 'Is it too late Donnald'? 'No aunty, it's never too late, get busy, and write it this evening. I've never admitted this to a soul, not even to myself. But I will tell it to you now. I was eaten up inside with jealousy, jealous of your mother, of her friends, I was possessive of her, being eight years older than her, I must have been thinking that I owned her. She dropped the bombshell when she told us of her plans to emigrate, I blamed Joan Considine for encouraging her, and sure she didn't have too'. 'There was nothing here. Don't be crying aunty; write that letter, mom will be happy to hear all about your feelings. Here's my hanky, dry your tears now love'.

'Something else Donnald, I've made a Will and I've left the little house and the piece of ground to whoever the Parish Priest of Saint Ann's is at the time of my death. I'm sure it will be handed over to the Bishop. Should I put that in the letter? Or should I change the Will'? 'Don't change the Will, mam wouldn't want it, she's gone so long'. 'But you Donnald, you're next of kin, you could sell it'? 'No aunty, leave it now as it is'. 'It's not the way it was when my sister left. I made changes. Taking out the post office savings I turned your granny's' bedroom into a knitting room. Two women joined me in the knitting; shelving was put in to hold all the wool and the knitted garments'. 'You'll have to show me aunty'. 'I will. I sold the rest of the land around it, and with that money I had water laid on, my bedroom was made more comfortable, I got a radiator put in, a fire range in where the open fire was, new windows, and a shed built for the turf'. 'Weren't you very positive'? 'I was and your mother was too. Our mam and dad didn't drive or beat anything into us; it was just the way we were. That's why I'm questioning my decision in keeping my Will the way it is by leaving the house to the priest, someone might move into it who wouldn't appreciate it'. 'Don't worry about that'. 'Here we are at the Saint Ann's Chapel'. 'My goodness isn't it quaint. Let's go inside, my it feels cold, this is where ye go to Mass'? 'I don't come down any more, there's no-one to bring me. It's here your grandparents got married, where we received our entire sacraments, poor Father Clancy he knew us all inside out'. 'I often heard mam talk about him, he wrote her a couple of times'.

'Take your photos; I'll say some prayers'. 'I'll go outside to get some good shots'. After a time Brid could hear voices. It was Father Tomson and Donnald coming in. 'Look who I met aunty'. 'Hello Brid, I've met your nephew, all the way from Texas'. 'Yes Father he is on holidays here in Ireland; he'll be heading up North in the morning'. 'Very good, come up to the house and we'll have a drink'. 'Thanks Father, we don't want to put you out'. 'Love to have ye're company, there's a good fire on'. The priest's house was a small neat cottage. 'What a lovely parlour Father'. 'Yes it's comfortable; I did a couple of alterations to it, putting my own mark on it. Sit down, what will ye have? How about a hot toddy'? 'Yes, I'll try one of them, how about you aunty'? 'I would love one. It's my usual night cap'. 'Now Father Tomson, I know a Tomson back in

Texas, we work in the same office. He would be one of the ten accountants there with me'. 'As a matter of fact, that's the business he is in'.

Small World

'It would be a long shot if it was my cousin'. 'It would be, what's your cousin's name? Wouldn't be Gerry by any chance'? 'For Gods sake, that's his name'. Was he here on vacation a couple of months ago'? 'He was home, I met him in his father's house in Cashel, they invited me over the evening they were having a get together in his honour, and his father Noel is my Uncle'. 'Sit there near aunty; I'll get a picture of the two of you and the lovely parlour. Well I will have something to tell him when I go back, it sure is a small world'. 'I'm sure you are finding it a bit of a challenge driving around these narrow roads in comparison with the wide open Texan highways'? 'A challenge it is'. 'Did you lose your way many times'? 'I think the worst time I lost my way here was at two o'clock in the morning when I ran out of gas (Donnald could see his aunty staring at him, a prayer in her heart, don't tell you stayed overnight there). At a little house some people were waiting for a cow to calve and that's why they were up so late'. 'Was the cow lowing, very loud'? 'She was'. 'That's the Ryan's'. 'Yes I think that was their name a very hospitable couple'.

(Change the subject Brid was saying to herself, change the subject for heavens sake). Then changing it herself, 'do you have many at Mass on a Sunday Father? Has the attendance gone down much'? 'It has Brid, but the Ryan's always come, in fact herself asked me up to bless the cow and twin calves. Two lovely calves, poor Eileen, innocent creator, named them Billy and Betty. Poor Eileen, she didn't get much of a chance in life'.

Father Tomson was on for a big chat. Brid grabbed her walking stick, 'Donnald I have to be home to take my tablets and it's an hour after time already. Thanks so very much for the hot toddy, we will see you soon again'.

'Aunty that was a sudden take off'. 'My heart was in my mouth for fear he would ask where you stayed that night and it would eventually lead up to that'. Father Tomson closed the door after them thinking to himself what a funny old woman, what a dart she took. 'Write the letter aunty and I'll make sandwiches for this evening's supper'.

After the meal and letter written and ready for posting. He went to see the knitting room and the story about all the knitting, a good few sets of caps, scarves and gloves were left, 'pick out what you like there Donnald, take to your mam and girlfriend'. 'Thanks aunty'. 'All the jumpers are gone I gave the last one to the district nurse, she comes to me every Friday all the way out from Limerick, brings me what I need in medicine and groceries so I gave her the jumper'. 'Why did you give up knitting'? 'Couldn't keep paying the women, taking some orders, paying a little each week, some moving away, others losing their jobs, and some people couldn't keep up their weekly payments, so I lost out on a lot of money, same way with the shops cycling into Limerick with the knitting garments was getting too much, I blame my hip trouble on it. Getting someone to stay with mam, who was bedridden, was getting harder, so I gave it up and I wasn't sorry'.

Donnald heads North

Morning came around at last. Brid had a good breakfast ready for Donnald and some sandwiches for along the way. 'Are you going straight to Dublin from here'? 'Limerick is first port of call Aunty, I must change that car for a bigger more comfortable one, get to a garage see what's on offer or I'll be walking around Dublin with my knees at my chest'. 'Donnald, you have a great sense of humour'. 'Thanks now for everything and I'll see you in three weeks time with your passport, so be packed and ready'. 'I will Donnald, good bye Donnald, safe journey'.

Listening to the car radio helped to shorten the road. The highway into the northern end of Ireland was a much easier picturesque drive than the streets of Dublin. The heat and space of this car was a real comfort. Who would know where Author O'Hara lived, his dad's oldest brother on the outskirts of Belfast? I'm almost sure I'm on the right track. Maybe I'll ask this man. Can you tell me where Author O'Hara's house is please Sir'? 'The next drive way on your right there'. 'Thank you'. I must slow down now, that looks like it. Boy, that's some house and what a driveway, flowers everywhere.

Standing admiring the great oak door he had already made up his mind he was at the wrong house. An elderly man with a walking cane opened the door slightly. 'Sorry to trouble you Sir, I'm looking for Author O'Hara'. 'That's my name, what can I do for you'? Looking at this man, Donnald thought he was looking at his father.

Margaret Dowling

Meeting his Father's Family

'I'm Donnald O'Hara, my dad was Stephen from these parts, he immigrated to Texas in USA back in....' 'Say no more young man I'm Stephen's older brother. You are his double uncle Author. Well where did he get a son the height of you? What height are you'? 'I'm six foot four'. 'Come in, I shouldn't be asking them kind of questions at the door. My wife is in the kitchen, we were just going to sit into dinner. Helen, look who we have here'. 'Who is that'? Helen was a plump white haired woman with the most welcoming smile. 'He is my nephew Donnald from Texas'. 'My, your brother Stephen's son? Let me reach up and welcome you. Come sit down, we were just about to have dinner'. 'I'm sorry, I won't intrude'. 'Stop Donnald, Helen always puts on too much food anyway. Sometimes the lads pop in; I always like to have something for them'. 'Who might the lads be'? 'Your cousins Donnald, you have three of them from this house, married with a few children each of their own. The oldest is Tom, he is into machinery, tractors, diggers, and the like, that have T O'Hara signs on them'. 'The very same'. 'You've seen them'? Thinking to himself they're well to do. I wonder what the other two are into. The dinner was left in front of him, all the vegetables and a fine thick steak. Conversation was about his dad, Texas and the life there. He found out his other two uncles were only a few miles from here. George was the nearest, lived in a bungalow, owns a big farm of land. They have two daughters and two sons. Sean is a couple of miles further on, he owns a menswear shop in Belfast. They have a son and daughter, the son works in the shop with him, and the daughter Angela is a teacher.

'And your two aunts, Betty married, has two daughters, she is Betty Fran Black in County Down and Delia, now a Mrs Howard, they have a son and daughter, the oldest daughter is a dentist. So there Donnald, eat up. There's a lot to meet'. 'Come on Author', says Helen fussing about the place, you can't keep Donnald all to yourself, you've phone calls to make, and tell them come over this evening'.

'I'll run upstairs and fix the spare bedroom for our guest. How long are you staying Donnald'? 'I've almost three weeks here if ye will have me'? 'Stay as long as you wish, my brother Stephen's son'. More hugs.

Helen comes into the kitchen, 'Donnald bring in your bag and I'll show you where to go'. The bedroom was fit for a king. 'Oh! Man' he thought, such a contrast to mam's side of the family, living wise. The bathroom is so rich. 'Now Donnald, if you want to shower and rest for a few hours your welcome to do so. Author is going to be busy on the phone now for a while'. On his own looking around he thought of his dad, dear dad, what a pity you never came back to see this. I know I'm going to enjoy this; they are so warm and welcoming. That Helen, she must be the mammy of them all?

Taking his shower and changing into fresh underwear, lying down on the bed with just a rug over him he drifted off to sleep. Next thing he knew Helen was standing over him with a tray of steaming hot food. 'Helen' he said, 'you didn't have to bring my dinner up to me'. With a hearty laugh she said, 'Donnald this is your breakfast'. 'My breakfast, but I just lay down'. 'You're alright Donnald, it's nine in the morning, take your time. Some relations called in last night but we would not disturb you, the journey was long, and you needed the rest. They're arranging a big family get together the weekend down in O'Hara's pub.' 'I'll have time to see around Belfast before that'. 'You will and Uncle Author will be with you, he'll like nothing better than showing you the sights'. 'That will be good, now I will see in reality what my dad used to be telling me about when I was young'.

Margaret Dowling

A Night in Donnald's Honour

Down in O'Hara's pub his cousin Andy was serving up drinks. Drying his hands he hurried over to meet Donnald. So many relatives to meet and all of them so friendly. The young cousins, climbing up on his knee as he sat down, their parents checking them to have manners.

Looking around the pub seeing some old photos he was intrigued. 'Aye', says Andy, in his deep northern accent, 'you've spotted the ones your dad is in as a young lad'. He got up to look more closely, carrying one of his smaller cousins on his shoulders. Big man, like me and I'm crying. Glass after glass was filled and emptied again and again. His camera was busy now. He never heard such beautiful accordion music in his life. Songs were sung. uncle George the farmer had a deep baritone voice. Aunts Betty and Delia were inviting him to County Down. 'I will, I'll make time to stay a while with each one of you. There's uncle George I will be there too'. Calling Liam, Betty says 'you must take your nephew to your menswear shop, let him pick some things out there for himself'. 'Ach now Betty, there's ne'er a garment in my shop that will fit this young man, but he is welcome to come and pick out what he wants'. The night was getting wild, drink flowing, songs sung, music playing, and dancing. As things started to ease down, Donnald was finding himself the centre of attention of his relations; they were in fascination of his Texan accent.

Describing the States, larger than life, one little cousin piped up 'is that why your so big cousin Donnald'? That caused a laugh. 'Amarillo has the world's biggest weekly cattle auction, even the Texans are astounded in the Panhandle, the canyons sprawl across several counties. A Texan steak weighs seventy two ounces; you can find Texans in Billybobs Barbeque competing with each other to see who can eat one the fastest to get a free dinner'. As he continued talking he found himself describing how he got lost in the hills and narrow roads of Ballygala. The drink was doing its job, everyone laughing as he told of his Bed and Breakfast in the wee farm house where the cow was roaring loud because she was about to calve. Somewhere along the line he stopped, thinking to himself had he said too much already, letting his mothers side down.

People were starting to go home; the ones with small children had already left. Back in uncle Author's he couldn't stop thanking him for the great night. 'We must thank you Donnald, I think this is the very first time we have ever had a full gathering of the family together'. Saying goodnight he couldn't wait to get his head down.

Time was going too fast, between visiting, sight seeing and more get togethers in Andy's Pub.

Goodbyes and Hellos

Goodbyes had to be finally said, promising them all invitations to his wedding next year when himself and Madeline would be getting married. Now he was on his way back to the Irish passport office to pick up his auntie's passport. Then call to Nora and Pete McInerny's in Roscommon. The address his mom gave him was still in his pocket.

Having a little trouble finding their house, mother told me to bring candy, she was sure Nora would have a few grandchildren. After ringing the doorbell he had time to look around. Nice little bungalow and neatly cut lawn. As Pete opened the door they stood looking at each other. 'A big man like you can only be from one place, Texas'? 'You're right, could you be Pete'? 'I am which one is your mother Joan or Mary'? 'I'm Marys' son'. 'God Bless you, come in. What are you doing in this neck of the woods'? Explaining about his trips North and South, telling Pete about the promise he had made his mother that he would look up Pete and Nora. At this Pete went quiet and put his head down. 'Nora passed away five years ago Donnald, that will be sad news for Mary'. 'I'm so sorry, have you children'? 'Yes we have nine, seven and a set of twins, two boys they are grown up now. Poor Nora she was a great mother, the ould cancer got her in the end. But here, let me make you some coffee'. 'Are you sorry you left Texas Pete'? 'No, I'm not; Nora missed Mary and the ho-down dancing. She set up square dancing here, I used to help her, it was a lot of fun, but with babies coming we gave it up. Your mother, poor Mary, herself and Nora and Joan Considine, she became Mrs Jake Tolby, they were the greatest, does your mother hear from her at all'? 'At Christmas time, I know Joan has three sons. Here Pete, a little bottle of Paddy, and some candy for the grand children'. 'You didn't have to do that Donnald, here I'll open it, give you a drop for the road'. 'No thanks Pete, I've already drank too much in the last three weeks'. After a bit, Donnald got up and said 'I'll be on my way, so sorry about your wife Nora'. 'I know that, will you be able to find your way to Ballygala'? 'I'm sure I will, once is enough to get lost there'.

Next stop Ballygala, looking into the back seat of the car, I must stop and buy a large bag for all those gifts and souvenirs, there's the sandwiches wrapped neatly by Helen, just as aunt Brid did for me, same thoughts, same kindness, though miles apart in so many ways. It was a lovely drive all the way; soon he would be coming in view of Saint Ann's Chapel, then on by the old mill, smiling to himself as he remembered bathing in the stream. Turning in the old road, something appeared strange. The little house, he thought, there were some boards nailed to the little gable end window. Driving into the neat little yard it became all too obvious, doors and windows boarded up, he sat he didn't know for how long. Then a car drove in behind him, out hopped Father Tomson, opening his car door he reached for Donnald's hand.

Aunty Breathes her Last Breath

'I'm so sorry Donnald, your aunty died Friday morning, she had just passed away as the district nurse came, your aunty hadn't unlocked the door, but the nurse had a key to it. She knew immediately she had gone just minutes before, the body was still warm'. Donnald couldn't stop crying. 'Come down to the house and I'll make you a drink. I can't let you into the house until the solicitor reads the Will. You will call on him before you leave Donnald'? 'No Father, it has nothing to do with me, that will be your job Father'. 'It will be my job? Why do you say that'? 'Aunty had her Will made long ago, so I'm not going to go against her wishes'.

'She is to be buried with her parents. Thanks Father, thanks for everything, I will visit the grave and then be on my way'. Shaking hands, getting into the car, he bade farewell to Ballygala with one last photo shot of two lonely graves.

Eileen feeling Dizzy

The geansai was coming on well, the back and half the front done, it was looking well, putting it down she felt dizzy. Too much knitting and not used to it, her eyes could be giving trouble. Outside searching for eggs she knew a hen was laying out there somewhere. Her head felt fine again, I hope I don't need glasses she thought.

Taking a break from it will give my eyes a rest. Doing a little knitting occasionally will get it finished, at the rate I'm going now it will be ages before it's finished. I wish these dizzy spells would stop, they're coming more often now, and I'm feeling sick with them. The two sleeves and the complicated part of the neck, then sew it up. I won't tell Mick how I feel, or he won't let me knit at all. Eating dinner one evening she had to leave, go outside and throw up.

'Are you alright Eileen'? 'I'm thinking I have a bad stomach bug, it has been coming on me slowly, on and off for weeks'. 'The sooner you see a doctor the better, I'll ready the trap in the morning to take you in, and you look so pale Eileen, go into bed and rest yourself'.

In the morning her head was so bad she could hardly get out of the bed. 'My poor Eileen, I'll help you'. 'I was never so sick Mick'.

Surprise for Eileen

'I've a little bag ready there, should I bring it with me in case the doctor sends me into hospital for tests'. 'Put it in the trap, please God you won't need it'.

Doctor Lyons waiting room was busy enough, but as two doctors were there, Eileen figured it wouldn't be long until she would be called. Right now the awful feeling of sickness had left her; she was nearly asking Mick to take her home again.

Deciding a good check up would do no harm and he might recommend a tonic. 'Lie up on the couch Mrs Ryan; I'll just do a little listening to your breathing, just a general routine'. After a bit the doctor said 'Alright, you can sit up now. Just a few questions Mrs Ryan, you say you're almost forty two'? 'Yes doctor' 'And you think you're in the change of life'? 'I'm nearly sure that is what's wrong with me'.

'You're very right there dear'. 'So I've nothing to worry about'? 'No, not for the next few months anyway'. 'And, what then doctor'? 'You will have your baby, you're a good four months gone, and have you felt your clothes getting tighter? Mrs Ryan please close your mouth'. All she could say was 'Jesus. But Doctor Lyons, we hadn't done it in years, only that one time'. 'Once is all you need'. 'Mick got so mad after that.' 'Why Mrs Ryan?' 'He wasn't well the next day with heart palpitations, after bed rest he was fine'. 'Is he with you'? 'He is in the waiting room'. 'Tell him to come in to me'.

Eileen went out for Mick, returning to the doctor's office saying 'He won't come near you to talk about that side of things. Sure that's the very reason we had no children all these years (he couldn't)'. 'How did you manage to get him going that one turn? No you don't need to answer that question. I'll call him in myself'. 'But doctor.....' 'No need to worry Mrs Ryan, we'll respect his shyness'.

Thinking to himself there must be something very serious wrong with Eileen, she's in there a long time. 'Mick, Michael Ryan'? 'Yes, that's me'. 'Step in here would you please'? Getting up off the seat he staggered. 'I knew it', he thought to himself. 'Is Eileen alright doctor? What's wrong with her'? 'I'll let her tell you herself. When was the last time you had a check-up Mick'? 'A few years ago'. 'I'm thinking you're due another one'. 'I'm alright, it's Eileen'. 'Take off your jacket; let me listen to your heart'. 'I've ould clothes on me, I'm not prepared'. 'Just your heart I want to hear, pull up your shirt good man, now deep breaths. Mick I would like you to come in for a general check up'. 'When doctor'? 'Within the next month, don't let it go any longer. I'll want to see you and Eileen in two months, take things easy now, her morning sickness should be passed by then'.

Out in the trap sitting up ready to take off. Mick looks anxiously at Eileen, 'are you going to tell me what he found wrong with you'? 'He did tell me I'm four moths pregnant'. 'What are you telling me'? 'I'm telling you that you are going to be a daddy'. Now, as she looked at him, there was that colour again, but a little deeper, 'are you alright Mick'?

'That happened the night you took leave of your senses and near killed me. I'm so looking forward to this little visitor; I wonder will it be a boy or a girl. Will you be alright Eileen'? 'I will, she says 'Sure aren't I a fine strong woman'? Thinking to herself; I wonder will you be?

Wobbling into the doctor's clinic for the two month check up. Looking at her he said 'your letting yourself get very big Mrs Ryan, lets see how this baby is coming along, if you get too big for a first baby and in view of your age you could be in for a hard time', thinking to herself 'it can't be any harder a time than poor cow Bessy had. 'Sit up on the stretcher', listening and listening here, there, then 'lie down Mrs Ryan', more listening, then he put his stethoscope down and sat looking at her. 'Mrs Ryan, he says, 'I don't know how I am going to tell you this (well she thought to herself, its not the baby for I felt life this morning) I know the reason your getting so big, I've found two heart beats'. 'You don't mean it'! Exclaimed Eileen, 'Its twins, how will I tell Mick'. 'Mick, he didn't come in for that check up. How did he take the news?' 'His face grew a strange shade of red, but he is very happy about the baby. Maybe I shouldn't tell him about the twins'. 'You must Eileen, for we will need to have you in a month ahead of time'. 'Really, doctor'? 'Yes not that there is any danger, just a precaution. Is Mick in the waiting room'? 'No, I couldn't face coming in the trap. A neighbour brought me in his car'. 'That's very sensible of you. But I do need Mick in here'. 'He won't come in now at all'. 'Why do you say that? 'Because he watches over me day and night, now with this news it will be worse'. 'Try to get him into me'. 'I will but I know it's hopeless'. Mick was putting in the cows as Eileen was getting out of the car. 'I'm just going to do the milking Eileen'. 'That's fine, I'll put on the dinner'.

After dinner was over, the conversation began. 'How's the baby coming on'? 'You had better sit down for this news. I'm having twins and both babies are doing well. Doctor Lyons wants you in for tests to do with your heart now; he thought that should shake you up and you might take it into your head and go into him'.

'Did you say twins Eileen, like the cow'? 'Don't compare me with the cow'. Keeping both eyes on his face she could see the colour creeping up.

'Well are you Mick'? 'Am I what'? 'Going for that check up'? 'As soon as all this is over, I will I have to be here with you for the baby, now babies'. 'The babies will need you more after they're born than they do now'. 'Go in and lie down Eileen'. 'I don't need to lie down, I'm going to try and finish knitting your geansai'.

Donnald goes Home to Texas

Packing gifts and souvenirs into a case, protecting them from breaking, chinaware, Belleck vases, a variety of glassware, bed and table linen, and greatest of all, photos of his dad in school, dressed in his football jersey, and many more, even of his grandparents. Now for the flight home, telling mom of aunty Brid's death and the way it happened was going to be hard, sending the passport back for him was sad too. However, it would be sadder if she died on the flight.

His mother and Madeline were waiting at the airport, his two favourite women. Barely looking at his mom he could just about get the words out, 'your sister Brid passed away about three weeks ago, I thought you would both meet, I was arranging to bring her over with me'. Putting her arms around her son, telling him 'you did the greatest charitable thing any son could ever do, we made our peace in our letters, I wrote back the very day I heard from her, you let her think it was I who sent you over and it all your own idea, you're a great son'. 'He is indeed Mrs O'Hara, if you don't mind; I'll cut in and welcome my fiancé back to me'.

'Now, now ladies, don't fight over me, or I'll go back again'. Feeling good at being back on home ground, he was looking forward to a real Texan meal, 'a pounder of pure beef burger topped with red onion, crushed garlic, red pepper, a side plate of mashed sweet potato and moms home made yellow corn bread, washed down by a large tankard of Budweiser'.

First Day back at Work

The first big job was to get the many rolls of film developed, that would take a few weeks. His first day back in the office, and looking forward to meeting Father Tomson's cousin Gerry. Crossing the floor, the two men with outstretched hands greeted each other. 'What a small world', they echoed. 'We have a lot to talk about, imagine your cousin the Parish Priest in my aunt's Parish of Ballygala'. Donnald found it difficult to get focusing on work. 'I'll have a strong mug of coffee, that should bring me down to earth'.

Opening up some of the gifts Donnald had brought back Madeline couldn't believe the beauty of the Royal Tara China, 'are these really for me she wondered. So many boxes of gifts' she exclaimed. 'Yes' says Mrs O'Hara, 'and all from his dads side of the house'. 'Oh! You can't say that, look at Brid's lovely knitted scarves and gloves'. 'Yes of course you're right there Madeline, God rest her now, she was a gifted knitter'.

The films will soon be developed, 'I'm sure Donnald will invite all the work mates over for an evenings viewing of the Emerald Isle, you'll be sure to invite your family Madeline'. 'I will and some of my work mates too, it's going to be a full house'.

An Irish Film Premier

Stocking up on food and drink, suggesting they should set up the Bar-B-Q outside to cook the beef burgers. Donnald agreed with that idea, and as he said, 'go one further hire a short order chef to do the cooking, that will give me time to remain on showing the films with cine camera'. Madeline agreed with that. Turning around she called 'Donnald', 'What is it'? he asked. 'It's your mother'. 'What about her'? 'She's crying'. Hurrying to his Mom he asked, 'are you alright? I know you're thinking of your sister Brid'. 'I am Donnald, but not alone that, it's poor Nora, rest her soul, I'm thinking about. She was so kind and full of humour. Nine children, including twins, no wonder she stopped writing to me, she didn't have the time. If only I knew I could have been better to her, poor Nora, the cancer to get her in the end'. 'Don't cry mom, why don't you write to Pete, tell him about your sister Brid, and the shock I got that evening after leaving him to find her dead and buried, while you're at it, write to Joan and Jake too, do that mom'. 'I will Donnald, I'll get started now'. 'Very good mom, Madeline and I are going to clear out the den, set it up for the premier of Irish film showing'. 'Oh Donnald, you're so funny'. 'Before you start letter writing, make a list of the friends you want to invite mom. The empty den looked big, but would it hold all they were inviting, his bosses, workmates, Madeline's friends from the hospital where she nursed, mom's friends and our neighbours'. 'I don't know Madeline, when we have chairs set up it won't be as big and a few small tables to hold drinks and ashtrays'. 'Could I make a suggestion Donnald, ask the guests not to smoke during the showing, it will be too congested'. 'Great idea Madeline, I'll put up a notice, excellent idea'. 'Donnald, it's going to be a great evening, your mom will be overcome when she sees her home on film. And, I'm dying to see you bathing in the old mill river in the nude'. 'Don't be naughty Madeline; there was no-one to take that visual scene'.

'Have you got a voice on the film while it's showing'? 'I'll have that all done before it starts. There's a few boys at work into camera work, so they will give me a hand with it'. 'Oh Donnald, I just can't wait for that Saturday to come round'.

Eileen in Labour

The smell of disinfectant and ether was enough to turn Mick's stomach each time he visited Eileen in the maternity ward. A month was a long time for him to be visiting a hospital, a place he had never been in his life time. Eileen was always in good spirits when he came to see her, except for today. Asking her if she was alright? 'I am' she answered, 'I went into labour this morning, so they will take me down to the delivery room soon'. 'Are you in pain'? 'I am and they're coming every three minutes. Here's one now, hold my hand Mick'. She squeezed his hand so hard he felt the sweat bubble out on his forehead. Then she relaxed. He was glad to see two nurses coming with a trolley. 'Now Mick' she said, 'I'm off to have our babies'. 'God bless you Eileen', he whispered.

A nurse showed Mick into the father's waiting room. He felt like a grandfather, instead of a new father, as he looked at the young waiting fathers sitting around talking and laughing.

He would keep to himself and pray for Eileen and the twins, 'his' wife having twins, who would believe it. Each time a nurse came into the waiting room he hoped it was for him. How long more would it take. One nurse came to him and told him his wife was doing well and the babies would soon arrive. As she left he wondered did the young fathers hear what she said. Thank goodness there were only two of them left now and they weren't talking to each other. He pictured himself to be the last one to get his news.

'Mick Ryan, congratulations, you're the proud father of a son and daughter', as he went to stand up, the floor went from under him. The next thing he knew he was in a bed with a lot of wires attached to him.

A nurse was mopping his brow. 'It's alright Mick, we will be bringing your wife in to see you shortly. The babies are doing well; they're sleeping now, so we won't disturb them'. Wheeling Eileen into the cardiac ward, the nurse explained to her, 'your husband had a mild heart attack. The doctor will talk to you about it later. It was lucky you were awake enough to tell us about his colour changing, you probably saved his life'.

'Hello daddy. How are you'? 'I'm feeling great just now. But how are you mammy'? 'I'm good, it will take a few weeks to pull up, I had a natural birth so that was good, the little boy is the dead image of you'. 'And the little girl, who is she like'? 'I'll say myself, but I don't know'. 'They'll be letting me out in a day or two, just a rest I need'. 'Mick, I'm saying nothing now, only for you to do what the doctor tells you. Mick, promise me'. 'I promise. I'm going to be kept in for nine days and I need that nine days'. 'Eileen, isn't that a long time'? 'Mick, I just had two big babies, weighing five pounds each. I have Gilbert Flannery of the garages phone number. I'll call them in the morning, tell them to keep an eye on the place they can do the milking and keep the milk'. 'Alright Eileen, if that's what you want'. I won't see you tomorrow, I have to rest. Nurse, take me back now please. Look after yourself Mick'.

Eileen has few Visitors

The nine days flew by quickly. Mick seen his twins, he was beaming and looked well, the doctor let him home after a week with a warning to take his tablets. Eileen's visitors were few; Mrs Flannery came in to see what she would need. Telling her she had left some baby things at the house and she thought Mick looked well. Gilbert would bring herself and the babies home later in the evening. She was so grateful to her and Gilbert.

Father Tomson was another visitor she had; he blessed herself and the babies. Then he sat on the side of the bed for a chat, telling her he had been talking to Mick and he seemed fairly good. His conversation turned to Donnald O'Hara's visit. 'He was in your house the night he went astray, wasn't that about the time the cow had the twin calves'. 'It was Father, exactly'. A few more words, then he enquired how old the calves were. 'I'm not sure right now, about a year I think'. 'I don't think they're a year yet Eileen'. 'Maybe not'. 'About nine months wouldn't you say'? 'I couldn't be sure, these two here are my big concern at the moment, and their Dad. Poor Mick, he is very excited over them'. 'Poor Mick is right. I bet he is excited alright, get in touch for the christening'. 'I will, thanks for coming in Father'.

Eileen was very busy dressing the babies with the help of a nurse for going home. A kind nurse brought in a big box of baby clothes. There's all sizes in it, you won't feel them growing into them. There are a couple of little white dresses; they could do for the christening. She was so grateful; she hoped there would be blankets and nappies too. While waiting for Gilbert to come for them she thought of her sisters. They didn't even know she was expecting, never mind that she had twins. Will I ask Gilbert to come by Kate's and I'll let her know? No, I'll leave it a day or two, the district nurse will be in twice a week for a while, I'll write a note, and she can drop it into Kate.

A big roaring fire greeted her as she walked in the door. Mick carried in one baby and Gilbert the other. 'You'll have a drink Gilbert'? 'Well, just the one, wet the babies' heads. God bless them, they are beautiful'. 'Thanks Gilbert for everything, not at all, thanks for the milk. It's the least we might do Gill'. 'The wife left a pile of baby stuff there, nappies as well; she'll come by in a couple of days to do a baby wash'.

Both babies were fast asleep, one at each end of the cradle that was placed in a corner by the fire. Eileen was looking around, 'Wasn't there a press there where you put the cradle Mick? Did you move that by yourself'? 'No, young Gilbert was here with me a couple of days, he is a great young lad, he did a lot of work for me. They're great neighbours Eileen'.

'I'm going to write a note for my sisters, I'll give it to the district nurse to leave it into them'. 'That's a good idea Eileen'. 'I'm going to bed for a couple of hours, the babies are not due a feed for at least three hours yet'.

Going into the room and looking at the bed before getting into it, she let a laugh. Mick went into see what was the matter. 'The new sheets, Mick, did you think it was the time to finally use them'? 'Will I did, young Gilbert helped me change the bed. I burned the ones I took off'. 'You did, what will we do for a change'? 'Gilberts mother brought these, they were her mothers RIP, but she never used them, had enough without them, she hoped you wouldn't mind taking them. Go rest yourself Eileen; you'll need a lot of it for I'm sure the nights will be hard going'. 'We'll face that when it hits us, call me when they shout'.

Mick pulled a chair over to the cradle and sat staring at his two little babies with tears in his eyes, 'will I be here to see ye grown up? I've had a couple of frights lately; it's the ould heart you know. I should take my tablets like the doctor told me to.

But I forget. Little Michael, she called you after me. Jane, I don't know where she got Jane from but I'm beginning to like it, Jane Ryan'.

The gentle tap, tap on her shoulder woke Eileen. She wasn't sure for a second where she was. Then Mick said 'your babies are awake'. 'Our babies Mick, their our babies'.

Mick feeds his Baby Son

The handy little gas stove she got from the Flannery's made all the difference for warming the bottles. 'Sit here Mick, hold your son like that and put the teat into his mouth'. 'Mammy, I never fed a baby in my life'. 'It will come easy. Just put that into his mouth, he will do the rest, and I'll feed her'. Burping and changing came easy. 'The little ones are tired; they should sleep until one in the morning'. As time went on Mick was gaining more confidence around them, only the worry was always there, when his colour changed to that dark red, 'are you taking your tablets Mick'? 'Aye, I am', 'I don't believe you Mick, and we need you'!

Eileen was relaxing for a while with a cup of tea in her hand, when it suddenly occurred to her Father Tomson asking about how old the calves were. Why did he want to know that? Funny questions to be asking me after I had twins myself, he didn't make a joke of it. Mick was talking of selling the bullock, maybe Father knows someone who will buy him, that's probably it.

'Are you selling the young bullock Mick'? 'I'm going to, we can use the money, I'll get a good price for him'. 'Anyone showing interest'? 'A few Eileen'. 'Is Father Tomson one of them'? 'No, why would he want a bullock'? 'I don't know, he was very interested in their age when he called to see me in the hospital. Just making conversation I suppose'.

Eileen sends Word to her Sisters

When Kate and Rita got Eileen's note they thought, 'well what a woman', 'God bless her, she'll need our help I'm sure' said Rita.
Telling the rest of the family there was twins in the Ryan household. Calling their brother Chris gave Kate a buzz. 'You'll be up to see her, don't expect too much, you know how she hasn't much. Rita and I are driving out to see her tomorrow, we have never been to see her or Mick before and this is one big occasion for our sister'.

Hearing the car drive into the yard Eileen thought the district nurse had come a day early. Seeing her two sisters, laden down with parcels coming out of the car. 'Well' she thought, 'that was quick'.
There was no time to look at Eileen, babies first, straight over to the cradle, 'that's Michael and this is Jane'. 'Look at Michael, he is a miniature Mick, God bless the two of them'. 'How are you Eileen'? 'Very good considering'. 'Why didn't you tell us you were expecting'? 'I was four months gone when I went to the doctor, because I was so sick, I was sure I had a fatal disease'. 'Well you are looking good now'. 'I feel good except for being tired, they are a month old and taking more of the bottle'. 'How is Mick?' 'The daddy, as a daddy, he couldn't be better, but his heart is bad, I don't know the minute he'll drop at my feet. Sit down, I'll make ye tea and tell ye all'. 'No Eileen, we'll make you tea. We brought you groceries from the cousins. There's tinned soup and can opener, we'll fix that for you and Mick'. 'Any for ye're selves'? 'No, don't mind us; we're here for the day to help you inside and outside'.

Sisters helping Out

'Say the word, we're at your command'. 'My good sisters, and after all this time'. 'Say no more Eileen, all that is past and gone'. 'Don't say anything to Mick that I was telling you about his heart, just look at his colour when he comes in'.

'Congratulations Mick'. 'Thanks and you're both welcome'. 'Well Mick, you can't deny the little lad, he is the image of you, bless them both'. 'It was good of ye to come out, Eileen did you make them a sup of tae'? 'Mick, you sit down there with Eileen and we will pour the soup for you'.

Looking at her two sisters over Mick's shoulder, there was concern in their eyes; Kate squeezed her lips and shook her head'.

'How are you feeling yourself Mick'? 'I think it is the excitement of the whole lot, but to answer your question Kate, I feel tired all the time'. 'I've the car out there, would you like me to drive you into see Doctor O'Boyle, and he might recommend a tonic'? 'It's kind of you Kate, I'll leave it until next week and I'll go in for sure. By the way that was lovely soup; I'll go out and do a few more jobs'. 'Very good Mick, we're here for the day so you don't need to worry'. 'He doesn't look good at all Eileen, he is a stubborn man'. 'Kate and Rita, I want you two to be godmothers for the twins'. 'Oh Eileen, it would be our pleasure and an honour to stand for your babies. I'll be godmother to Michael Junior' smiled Kate looking in to the cradle 'and I will have little Jane', Rita cooed.

'Would you like us to ask Uncle Chris to be one of the godfathers'? 'Indeed yes, but I couldn't invite my brother and his doctor wife into this squalor'. 'Now Eileen, your sister-in-law is the most down to earth person you ever met, your brother Chris would never have married her otherwise' says Kate, 'who will be the second godfather'? 'Gilbert Flannery, they're so good to us, I couldn't pass him up. I'll have the christening in a couple of week's time'. 'You'll be much stronger then, we will make up your bed for you Eileen, rest for a while before your dinner'. As

Kate went into the room, looking at the bed she was appalled at the sight of it, calling her sister Rita. Looking at the state of the bed they both shook their heads. 'Eileen a stor, we're looking at the bed'. 'I know, I know, it's not fit for a dog to lie on'. Kate making the suggestion as gently as she could, 'I have my mother-in-laws bed Eileen, I could get Frank and Tom to bring it over, it's in good condition'? 'Why are you crying Eileen'? 'I'm so embarrassed'. 'Don't be one bit, we are your family' consoled Rita. 'I'll stay and cook the dinner, Kate will get the men to bring the bed and in no time you and Mick will have an almost new bed, sure ye deserve the best'.

A Nostalgic Irish Film

The day after Donnalds Irish Film showing was over; mother and son had a little time together to chat about it, especially his father's part of the country. 'If only dad had made one trip home, just to see how they were, their beautiful homes and just everything about them'. 'Donnald, what did you think of your mothers side of the country'? 'Beautiful countryside mom, as you seen in the film, but weren't ye poor by comparison'? 'We were, but we never went hungry'. 'You must have invited the entire company to see where your roots come from'. 'It wasn't to be like that mom, but each one asked another friend, how could I say no'. 'It was a credit to you, the fine job you did filming the mountains, lakes and the wide green fields'. 'How could you have seen all that mom? You fell asleep at the Giants Causeway'. 'Now Donnald, that's not fair of you'. 'Mother the whole trip was one great experience for me. I'll see you sometime tomorrow, Madeline and I are going to take in a show tonight after work. Bye, see you', he give's her a gentle kiss.

Donnald was settling back into the normal way of things. Until the day he came home from his business in a steaming hurry. Straight into his bedroom, and banging the door behind him. His mother had never seen Donnald like this in her life. Standing outside his bedroom door she made a few attempts to knock and go in. She was in a state of worry. Himself and Madeline must have had a falling out and yet it couldn't be that because Madeline is working in theatre today. This early in the day they wouldn't be in contact with each other at all.

Donnald Upset

Without knocking she opened the door and went in. Donnald was sitting in a chair, his head between his hands. 'Dear God Donnald, are you sick'? 'No Mom, I wish I was'. 'What is it son? Tell me'. 'Gerry Tomson said a nasty mean thing to me in the office today and I'm very sure some of the office workers could have heard him. It seems the house in Ballygala' 'The Ryan's, yes I heard you talking about them'. 'Well, Mrs Ryan is after giving birth to twins and in the twenty years they're married they never had any children and now nine months after my visit she has twins'. 'But son isn't that a great blessing, what can it have to do with you? What did Gerry say'? 'He came over to my desk and said 'I believe you left a package after you in Ballygala, in fact I hear its two packages you left'? 'I couldn't follow him, so asking him what he was talking about. He says the house you stayed at, the woman is just after giving birth to twins and you're supposed to be the father.

Mom, I'm ruined; I'll loose Madeline, my job, the lot. 'What did you say to that ignorant guy'? 'I belted him across the face'.

A Nasty Rumour

'Listen mom, I'm going to go to my lawyer, explain what has happened and get him to draw up an affidavit. I will go straight back to Ireland and challenge the man I know who has started this scandalous rumour. Can you imagine how it must be for the Ryan's, if this rumour is going around their village? Your sister Brid, RIP was the wise old lady, now I see what she meant by saying don't get in too deep conversation with Father Tomson. I'm going back and have my good name cleared and that of the Ryan's too'. Madeline quickly arranged her hospital hours and insisting on travelling with Donnald, she said 'I love you and I will travel all the way with you'. 'I'm glad you're going over together. Did you tell your boss about the upset'? Mrs O'Hara wanted to know. 'I told him I had some business to settle in Ireland and need a few days leave, he just nodded his head, and take all the time necessary' was all he said. No doubt he has heard the rumour too'.

Sitting on the plane Donnald said' I didn't think I would be making a return trip this quick. I'm sorry Madeline you are coming under such circumstances'. 'Don't worry Donnald, we will face it together'. 'My lawyer, Mr Crawford has a friend in Limerick, a Mr Keer, a noted solicitor, he advised me to go straight to his office and give him this affidavit and he will take it from there'.

Changing baby Michael, Eileen heard the wheels of a car crunching on the stones in the yard. Smiling she said to herself the nurse is right on time. Greeting Eileen in her friendly voice she peered into the cradle, seeing only one baby she enquired where baby Jane was. 'My sister Rita took her home with her, she is going to mind her for a while, give me a little relief. Could you call to Rita's house to see the baby, at your own convenience of course'? 'I will, be sure Eileen, who knows I might get a hot one from Kate'? 'Sure I can make you one if you like nurse'? 'No, no Eileen, I'm only making a joke, you have enough to do and look after his lordship here. I didn't see Mick and I coming in, is he alright'? 'No, he is in hospital again, two days ago he took a bad turn, he looked bad, it frightened me, he dropped to the floor. Thank God, my two sisters were here, Kate rushed him into hospital. Rita said she would take one of the babies so I gave her the little girl, she is the quietest. He was doing well, Nurse Dea, taking his tablets and all'. 'Oh, I am sorry Eileen'. Standing in thought for a while, 'is something wrong nurse'? 'I was thinking would Mick have heard the nasty rumour'? 'Nasty rumour, what rumour nurse'? 'I was making a house call to an old woman in the village, she's a bit of a gossiper, I would much rather not see her at all, but it's my duty to visit everyone. Sit down Eileen, I'll make you a strong drink, you will need it and maybe I'll have one myself, although I shouldn't'. 'What are you mumbling about nurse, you're not like yourself at all'?

'I don't want you to take it personal Eileen'. 'It's about me, and then what can it be'? After a long pause and choosing her words as careful as she could, she said 'The young man from Texas stayed here one night, is rumoured to be the babies father'. Eileen sat staring into space for what seemed an eternity. 'I'm hearing things nurse, things that couldn't be further from the truth'. 'Do you think that young man knows this rumour, is going around'? 'If he does he will think I'm spreading rumours to get money out of him. What am I to do'? 'Your brother in Cork, who is a solicitor, he would give you good advice'. Eileen thought about this. Nurse Dea looking at Eileen thought she would have cried but then she has been through so much maybe the poor thing is cried out. 'Now Eileen, I must run, the baby is all changed and powdered down, I will call to your sister Rita to see baby Jane'. 'Thanks nurse'. Eileen appeared to be in a daze as Nurse Dea let herself out. Sitting by the cradle, looking at baby Michael who was the image of his poor dad, who was now in hospital.

It took Eileen a long time to pull herself together, the worst thought she had, 'was it said to Mick? Would he then be of the same thinking'? Reaching for the bottle of Paddy she had bought months ago out of the hundred pounds, making a hot toddy for herself she sat down to cry.

Eileen meets her Brother

Sitting on her own, glass in hand, tears rolling down her cheeks, baby Michael fast asleep. Talking to herself 'where will I turn dear God'? So engrossed in the depths of her misery she didn't hear the car drive into the yard until the door opened and her sisters, Kate and Rita, walked in and a man behind them who looked familiar to her, yet for an instant she wasn't sure. 'Chris' she cried, 'that's right sister', and wrapping his arms around her he held her tight. 'You've been crying Eileen, we know the reason why, an ould fellow with too much drink on him in the pub was mumbling about a rumour into my ear' says Kate, 'it's about a sister of yours up the country, she had twins to a young Texan. My husband Frank nearly cleaned the floor with him. I had to stop him to get the real information out of the ould lad, only sorry thing he couldn't remember where he first heard it'.

'It was the district nurse that broke it to me when she called this morning to see baby Jane'. 'We phoned Chris and told him, he being a solicitor and all, he knows someone who would take this case and find the culprit, land them in jail for the rest of their days'. 'It's so good to see you, my baby brother Chris'. Tears in his eyes, 'I'm sorry sis it has taken so long. I seen baby Jane, she's beautiful and that little man over there, what a handsome little chap'. 'Here, let me make a cup of tea for ye' says Eileen. 'There's another car stopped outside' remarked Kate, 'there's three people in it. Would you believe it? It's Brid O'Brien's, may she rest in peace, nephew, he has a lady with him, you remember himself and his Aunt were in our pub the evening yourself and Mick were doing a bit of shopping'. 'I remember well, why is he here now'?

A Necessary Return

Touching down once again in Shannon airport, only this time in disturbing circumstances, he was in no form to point out the scenic beauty of the land to Madeline. The views he relished on his maiden trip, no it was different this time. With their overnight bag they hopped on a bus for Limerick. Madeline looking out the window as they travelled the bus journey, Donnald wondering in his mind 'is she thinking I am the father of those twins, no Madeline would never think like that about me, I hope'.

Entering the old fashioned offices of Mr Kerr, wondering to himself what views this man would have on such a hideous matter. Shaking hands with Donnald and Madeline, Mr Keer put them at their ease instantly. 'You know what your dealing with here Mr O'Hara, defamation of character, not only for you and the children's parents, but also the babies as they grow up a stigma would be on their name, you are doing the right thing, to nip it in the bud. Let me see the papers you brought from your lawyer Mr Crawford and Company, I see Mr Crawford has a letter drawn up here for Mr and Mrs Michal Ryan's signatures. I'm satisfied all papers are in order. We'll go in my car to the Ryan family home now. Do they know this unpleasant rumour Mr O'Hara'? 'Not from me Mr Kerr'. Driving in the cobbled stoned yard, noticing a very expensive Mercedes car parked at Eileen's door, Donnald said, 'I'll go in first'. 'And I will come with you Madeleine' offered. 'That's ok by me' agreed the solicitor, 'give me the nod when you want me to come in'.

Knocking on the door, at the same time Eileen looked out the window to see what Kate was talking about. 'It is him and there is another man sitting in the car'. 'Oh God help me, what can they want'? 'Easy Eileen, sit down, we're here to look after you' consoled her brother.

Answering the door Kate looked at Donnald, 'it's Donnald isn't it'? 'Yes it is and this is my fiancé, Madeline O'Reilly'. 'We're pleased to meet you, won't ye come in. You must have a very good reason to come all this way so soon again' says Eileen as she wiped down the table, hoping to hide her nervousness. 'Yes, I have a good reason' announced Donnald. Eileen handed each one a cup of coffee and a piece of cake. Then looking straight into Donnald's face, 'it's the nasty rumour isn't it'? 'Yes it is, you already know then'? Rushing on with her words, 'I didn't put out that rumour, people might think I did, to try and get money out of a rich American. I know there are people here that look down on Mick and myself because we're poor. Our baby son is the picture of his father', jumping up from the chair her fists closed tight she shook them at the ceiling, she swore as sure as her name was Eileen Ryan she would murder the person who spread such scandal. Kate and Rita put their arms around her and sat her down, Chris putting his hand on her shoulder saying 'hush, Eileen, hush dear girl. We're all here to support you. Now, let's hear from Mr O'Hara'. 'Don't mind the mister, call me Donnald. Eileen, I know only too well you're not looking for money from me. Let me tell you about Father Tomson's cousin Gerry who works in the same office as me, he thought he had a great joke saying in earshot of the office staff that I fathered twins in Ireland, only he didn't express it in as tactful a term. Eileen, I landed Gerry one punch in the jaw, it knocked him right across the floor, it took the office staff to pull me off him'.

'When I was in hospital Father Tomson came into see me and the babies, I thought it odd he to ask me how old the twin calves were, I said about a year old, he says I think they're more like nine months, it passed and I thought no more about it until a couple of weeks later, I said to myself, that was a peculiar question Father Tomson asked me, then it went out of my head entirely'.

'It's a thousand to one that Father Tomson should have a first cousin working in the same company as me. When I go back I don't know if I'll have a job or not, this is my fiancé here, Doctor Madeline O'Reilly, I know she's very upset and my poor mother also, her sister Brid, may she rest in peace, had no time for Father Tomson, but she gave me no reason. I have a solicitor with me, he is sitting out in the car, I've a letter and documents drawn up Eileen, Mr Keer will witness you signing them to say I'm not the children's father'. 'Oh! Donnald, you went to all that trouble'. 'It's no trouble; our good names have to be cleared, also for the sake of the twins'. 'Tell Mr Keer to come in'. Chris called Donnald as he went to the door, 'would that be JJ Keer'? 'That's his name, do you know him'? 'Well, we are in the same profession; I was in university with him, it's a small world. I'll sit in a secluded corner until the business is taken care of, then I'll show my face' Chris whispered. At the door Donnald turned around to Eileen, 'I haven't seen Mick, is he out on the land'?

Signing the Paper

'**N**o Donnald, Mick wasn't well with his heart, we're afraid he heard this awful news and took bad, and he is in hospital'. 'I'm sorry Eileen'.

Introducing Mr JJ Keer to Eileen, 'he will show you the papers drawn up'. Shaking hands with Eileen and remarking on this unfortunate business, Mr Keer proceeded to explain the details of the letter that Donnald had drawn up by his lawyer, Mr Peter Crawford in Texas. Eileen was quite willing to sign. The business concluded, they were about to leave when Chris came out of the corner, 'Good day to you JJ'. 'What, why it's Chris Downes, long time no see'? 'It sure is, you've met my sister Eileen, disgusting business this'. 'Don't worry, we'll set it right'. 'By the way JJ, wouldn't you want Mr Ryan's name on there too'? 'Would it be alright with Mrs Ryan if we did pay a visit to the hospital'? 'I will go with ye' says Eileen, 'I need to see him, he is in two days now. We'll try not to upset him'.

Just wakening up from a sleep, Mick felt very well until his mind recalled what he overheard two people saying in the local shop. He wasn't sure if they had seen him. All he could remember was sure he's not the father of them twins at all; it's that big Texan that was here some months back. Getting his few bits, he hurried away on his bike. As he reached the house he had his mind made up to challenge Eileen. As he reached the house Kate's car was in the yard. He wouldn't say anything until she was gone. The last he remembered was his hand on the latch of the door, the next he knew he was been wheeled in here with these wires all over his chest again. Where is Eileen? Is it true? He knew in his heart it wasn't, but he needed her reassurance. Sure the little Michael, my very own double.

Another Fright

Lifting his head to look towards the door, Eileen was standing there in her lovely blue coat. 'Hello Mick, you've given me another fright. What am I going to do with you? Mick my love, what brought it on this time'? She could see the tears welling up in his eyes. 'You heard a nasty rumour'? Nodding his head, he reached for her hand. 'Mick, I've Donnald here and a solicitor from Limerick and my brother Chris is with them, you don't mind? They want to talk to you, I'll bring them in'.

Looking a bit embarrassed, 'relax Mick' says Donnald, 'meet your brother-in- law Chris Downes, he is in the legal business as is this man who's representing me, Mr JJ Keer'. Explaining the unfortunate affair to Mick, they could see his face brightening. Just then his doctor came in; 'you will have to wait outside for a few minutes'. As the doctor came out, Chris stayed back. 'I would like to have a word doctor, how is my brother-in-law'? 'He is your brother in law? Well, Michael Ryan has serious heart valve blockage'. 'What are his chances of a successful bypass'? 'Well, it can go good or bad, but in his case it could be very successful seeing as he is a non smoker and for his age in very good health otherwise'. 'Have you heard the name Doctor Lisa Moran'? 'I was at medical school with a Lisa Moran'.

Mrs Ryan has her Say

'She could be very well my wife, she is a heart specialist in Cork General Hospital, right now, perhaps we could do something for Mick, and money is no object'. 'I will check with Dublin right away, he could be on his way in an ambulance this evening'. Chris thanked the doctor and went into see Mick, who had just finished signing the official form. 'Isn't that good news Mick' says Eileen. 'It is now I can die a happy death'. Chris laughing, 'there's no sign of death about you'. Then looking at Eileen, 'did you arrange the babies christening'? 'I will, I'll talk to Kate and Rita when I go home'.

In the car Mr Keer said 'our next call is Father Noel Tomson, he has some signing to do also'. Donnald wanted to know if he would be at his house now. 'He is usually there of a Friday evening' Eileen answered.

Driving into the yard Mr Keer tutored Eileen in what to say. 'Mrs Ryan, you will go before us, ring the door bell'. 'Where will ye be'? asked Eileen anxiously. 'Right behind you. When he opens the door, all you have to say is Father Tomson; these men wish to have a word with you. Then we will walk in behind you'. Eileen was glad of her new blue coat and scarf; she must remember to tell Donnald she got it out of his hundred pounds.

Looking startled at first, then blushing, then realisation hit him, Father Tomson turned pale. Eileen was sure he was going to faint. Saying 'come in', in a whisper, he led them into the parlour. 'Please sit down, can I get you anything'? Ignoring the question 'Father Tomson, this is Mr JJ Keer, through my own lawyer in Texas who arranged for this man to be a witness to the signatures on these documents. We would like you to read through these. This is Mr Chris Downes, Mrs Ryan's brother, who is also in the same profession'. After reading over the papers he looked up at them, still with the pale colour. 'You're asking a lot of me, by asking me to make that apology at Sunday mass'. 'Either that or a courthouse to clear our names of this slander'.

'You want me to stand on the altar and say that I spread a damaging rumour about the Ryan's and their baby twins and caused Donnald O'Hara grief by passing the same scandal to my cousin Gerry who works in the same accountancy firm in Dallas Texas. Don't expect me to do that'. 'I hope Father Tomson you realise I'm in danger of losing my job. The Ryan's have already suffered as a result of this horrendous rumour, Mr Ryan has suffered a heart attack, and is in coronary care, and those children must go through their life with a stigma hanging over their heads'.

'Mrs Ryan, have you anything to add'? 'The day Father Tomson visited me in hospital he was curious as to the age of the twin calves'. 'Thank you, that's all. Now what is it to be'? 'I will, I'll apologise from the altar in my own words'. 'Not good enough, you must start with what is written before you'. 'My Bishop will be on to me. I am deeply sorry, it was only to Gerry I said it'. 'Well, there was no reason for you to discriminate your parishioners. Now has my aunt Brid O'Brien's Will been read to you'? 'It has', 'You know the contents'? 'I do'. 'This is for you to sign in my presence that you lay no claim to said property, it will be returned to Miss O'Brien's nearest relation, Mr Donnald O'Hara etc, in the absence of his mother. Thank you, any reneging in these agreements will result in a court case'. 'Anything else'? 'Oh, yes, Mr O'Hara will be at Mass Sunday to hear your apology. Good evening to you Father'. Now, I'll leave you at Ryan's. Donnald thank you and I'll pick up Madeline; leave you to your car'.

Eileen had something else on her mind, Kate. 'Mick wants the babies christened but I'm not taking them to that man in St Ann's'. We've everything ready in a bag thanks to Mrs Flannery; we found the two little christening gowns. We'll bring them with us Eileen and iron them up, arrange with the hospital chaplain for the christening'. 'When do you think that will happen'? 'We'll try for Sunday'. 'Oh! I wish I knew it before Donnald and Madeline had gone'. 'Don't worry about that, they're staying in a B&B in Limerick tonight, but they're coming around to the pub for a night cap later. We'll pick yourself and baby Michael up in the morning so you'll have tomorrow to relax, how do you feel now Eileen'? 'I can't believe so much could happen in one day, I'm feeling great. I'll feel better Sunday after the babies are christened and Father Tomson has explained himself to the parish. Kate, Rita, during the week I was talking to Gilbert Flannery and he is always ready with good advice. I mentioned to him I want to sell out lock stock and barrel, I know Mick wont ever be able to work the land again, and I'll take whatever offered'. 'Don't be soft Eileen, hold out for as much as you can get, where will you go'? 'I've no idea yet'? 'You'll never be stuck while I'm in it' says Rita.

'Gilbert has a buyer for the cattle already. Good night now, have a good nights sleep. By the way Kate, I never thanked you for the bed, such comfort, I couldn't get to sleep the first few nights'. 'Go on yourself Eileen. You'll be sure to call to Gilbert on your way down, tell him about the christening Sunday'.

Calling in to Gilbert, Mrs Flannery opened the door. 'Hello Mrs McGovern, please come in'. 'Thanks, but I can't'. Relaying Eileen's message for Gilbert. 'We'll be there don't worry, Eileen will see you herself on Sunday'. 'You will be going to Mass in St Ann's on Sunday Mrs Flannery I hope, it should be interesting, no harm to put the skids under him, he is known to spread gossip about people in our parish. His Bishop will hear about this, mark my words'.

Father Staunton, the hospital chaplain was a gentle elderly man, making a great fuss of the babies. Both sets of godparents were present, Madeline, Mrs Flannery and Chris's wife Lisa also came. Most important was the daddy in his new shirt and Eileen's hand knitted grey geansai. After the baptismal ceremony was over a meal was prepared for the party in the staff dining room. Mick was beaming with pleasure.

Mick a new Man

A chance to have a quiet talk with Eileen. 'Did you hear the news'? 'What news'? 'They're taking me to Dublin in the morning to have a heart by-pass done; they tell me it's the best heart hospital in Europe. Now Eileen, I could live to see my children grown up yet'. 'You will Mick, you will', she didn't mention she was planning on selling out. Wait until the by-pass operation is over. Donnald and Madeline were saying their good-byes. Taking Eileen to one side Donnald told her about his Aunt Brid's little house, it was now his and he was handing her the keys, 'move in at your convenience, it's fully furnished, centrally heated, running water and electricity, there's a garden back and front and a shed. Your good friend Gilbert Flannery will move you into it when you like'.

Eileen was speechless, 'but Donnald why'? 'Ask no questions, its due time you all had comfort. Madeline and I are getting married next July, you will get our invitation, and if you decide to come the cost will be taken care of'. Eileen stood up, 'whatever can I say, I cried all day Friday, today I'm ready to stand on the rooftop and sing'. Donnald and Madeline waved as they went out the door. Chris and his wife Lisa came to say goodbye also. Eileen looking at her sister in law, 'had you something to do with Mick going to Dublin for a heart by-pass'? Smiling she said, 'We take care of our own. Bye now and good luck in Donnalds Auntie's house'. It was a good day. Mick was happy to have seen young Michael and Jane baptised.

We're Back

Touching down in Dallas, it was a happy Donnald and Madeline. Opening his mother's door, calling 'Mother, we're back', running from the sitting room to greet her son, he lifted her into his arms. 'Donnald put me down and tell me the news'. 'Make some coffee and be prepared for a long story'.

'Thank God, it worked out so well for you and that poor family got my old home, what a great thing to happen, you're such a generous son'.

Back in the office, no one passed any remarks about anything, only difference was a new man sitting at Gerry Tomson's desk. A letter from Eileen told him Mick's operation was a big success, they gave him at least another twenty years, the babies are creeping around your aunty Brid's lovely floor. We've sold Mick's place and now we have a nice nest egg. Before I close, no-one knows where Father Tomson went, we have a lovely man in his place Donnald. See you at your wedding.

PS I'm learning to drive a car now.

THE END